I0620412

The Zrakon's

Bride

Shifters of Scotland

Linda Barlow

Linda Barlow Books

Linda Barlow Books
www.lindabarlow.com

Publisher's Note: This is a work of fiction. Names, characters, places, and incidents are a product of the author's imagination. Locales and public names are sometimes used for atmospheric purposes. Any resemblance to actual people, living or dead, or to businesses, companies, events, institutions, or locales is completely coincidental.

Book Layout ©2013 BookDesignTemplates.com

The Zrakon's Bride/ Linda Barlow -- 1st ed.
ISBN: 9780989307086

Beauty Meets Her Beast

Are maidens still sacrificed to sea dragons? Kate Beaton is a lover of folklore tales about beauties and beasts, maidens and monsters, princesses and frogs. But when she visits a quaint Scottish village, she is surprised to find that they take the ancient legends seriously.

Ross Malloch is a modern Highland laird with a family secret—there have been shape shifters at Mallochbirn for centuries. The Zrakon is in his blood. And on Midsummer's Eve, the only thing his alpha male sea dragon can think about is finding his one true mate.

The Zrakon's Bride is a short, erotic paranormal romance from Rita award-winning romance author Linda Barlow. It is intended for mature audiences.

Chapter One

Ross stood on the ancient battlements of Mallochbirn Castle, looking out over the churning waters of the sea. The day was stormy and warmer than usual. Humid. The skies were leaden and heavy with rain. His eyes searched the rocks, the crags, the distant headlands, and, most of all, the rough, white-capped waters surrounding his tiny island in northwest Scotland. "Come to me," he murmured, over and over. "I summon thee. Come."

The words were spoken without his volition. Oh, he knew he spoke them, and understood their meaning, but it wasn't his rational mind that had driven him up into the tower and out to the crenellated battlements. He spent most of the year resisting all thought of the ancient legends of Mallochbirn. Yet here he was, following the dictates of the tale, like many a fool before him.

How many generations of his family had stood here, on the worn stone, sending their souls out of their body, restlessly questing, seeking something they yearned for but could not name? He glanced up at the great stone dragon, symbol of Mallochbirn and his family, carved in weather-smoothed basalt atop the highest tower. His dragon. His doom.

A sleepy sea gull flew in, cawing. Ross locked eyes with the creature, which wheeled and flew away, fast. "Not you." He watched the bird as it became smaller and smaller. Soon it was nothing more than a speck on the horizon.

The waves rolled in, breaking and hurling their salt spray high on the rocks into which the old fortress was anchored. Ross felt the waters, into them, under them. Plenty of life there, but not the life he sought. Nothing stirred except the pounding and churning of water upon ancient rock.

A loud crack of thunder jolted him. *Idiot*, he said to himself. He stood there for some time longer, buffeted by the wind, watching the storm sweep in from the sea. Jagged bolts of lightning lit up the sky, and the air sizzled with the power of the raging elements. He knew he ought to go inside instead of making himself a target for the lightning, but some defiant spirit kept him there, absorbing Nature's ferocity.

His vision, sharper than usual, caught an unusual movement on the causeway that led to the island. The

gravel roadway there had an inch or two of surf breaking over it. The tide was receding, but the winds had
whipped up waves, and causeway wouldn't be safe until
the water backed off completely. He leaned forward
over the retaining wall, trying to get a better look. No
cars were allowed on the island. What fool was at-
tempting to drive over?

Nobody local would even dream of doing such a
thing. Particularly on this day of the year—the morning of Midsummer's Eve. It must be someone who did
not belong on the island or in the village. A stranger.
But this was a place where strangers were not allowed.

Ross stalked into the tower and down the long,
winding staircase that led to the main part of the castle. He wished someone had installed an elevator. Maybe it was time for a few more renovations around here.

He caught the intruder getting out of the car on the
narrow stony beach where the end of the causeway met
the rocks of the island. The dark-clad figure was considerably shorter than Ross was, but not until he
slipped behind and applied the edge of a fine Scots dirk
to a slender throat did he realize the intruder was female.

She tensed, but did not panic. "Whoa," she said.

"Reckless to be disregarding all the signs," Ross
said. He was trying to stay loose, ready for anything.
The intruder was clad in light clothing suitable for a
cool summer in northern Scotland. His dirk was prob-

ably unnecessary, but he wasn't fool enough to under-estimate her because of her sex. "If you were to drown, no one would be surprised."

"A slashed throat would be investigated," said the intruder—American, by her accent.

"You'd be surprised at the injuries than can be inflicted by some of the razor-sharp rocks hereabouts. Who are you?"

"My name's Catriona Beaton. People call me Kate. And you are?"

"Angry. Trying not to be careless with this blade, but no guarantees. I'd advise you to remain still, like a mouse." He patted her down efficiently with one hand and found nothing. Except some appealing curves.

"Hey, I'm harmless," she protested.

Ross turned her loose with a shove and sheathed his blade.

She straightened and rubbed her neck. Ross estimated her to be somewhere in her twenties, with dark hair, regular features, and a strong, fit body. The young woman's dark hair was swept up in an intricate style with little wisps of curl framing her features. One lock, though, had escaped its confinement to drift haplessly down the side of her throat. Her eyes were the light, clear green of sun-drenched tropical seas. They were rimmed with dark, soft lashes and arched with feathery eyebrows to which he would love to touch the

tip of his tongue. She had a stubborn chin and distinct-
ly kissable lips. Those lips were arched up in a smile.

"Are you the owner of this place? Mr. Malloch?"

"This place and most of the surrounding land, aye.
You're trespassing."

"Sorry about that. I was hoping to meet the laird."
She was gazing curiously at the knife he had sheathed
in a leather casing on his belt. "Do you always wear a
sword? Isn't that a little anachronistic?"

"It's a dirk. It's useful for confronting gatecrashers.
You're lucky your car wasn't swept out to sea. What
you did is not only forbidden, but also dangerous."

"Forbidden?"

"No cars are allowed on the island. That's one reason why the causeway isn't paved." He gestured to the
stony dirt road that was becoming visible as the surf
continued to retreat. The local vicar's orange cat was
prowling near the water line, looking impatient. He
must have crossed to the island at low tide and gotten
stranded here. He fussed over that cat occasionally,
which he probably shouldn't do, since it encouraged
him to visit.

"There aren't many cars in the village, either," he
added. "We don't like to pollute our pristine sliver of
Scotland with modern chemical fumes."

"I noticed. The whole village seems anachronistic,"
she said cheerfully. "Or have I stepped through a time
warp into the past?"

She had an engaging smile and a pleasant way about her. He had to school himself to resist her charm. "Why are you here?"

"I've come to speak to the laird. I emailed, but received no reply. Is email another of the modern conveniences you disdain, Mr. Malloch?"

She was clearly guessing, but he decided not to deny his identity. "I'm not receiving guests. The tide is falling, so it should be safe enough for you to turn your car around and return to wherever you came from."

"I came all the way from Boston. You know—far off in the New World?" She grinned at him.

"Why? What do you want here? Few people in the States have ever heard of this place."

"I know. It's amazing how quiet you've kept it. Why is that?"

"Why did you say you were here? Who do you work for?"

"No one. I'm a writer, doing some research."

He was skeptical. "I thought research was conducted on the internet these days."

"You can get lots of documents online, but for some material you still have to visit libraries. And the only way to talk to people is to get out there and meet them."

"Maybe some people don't want to meet you. Ever thought of that possibility?"

"Even if I'm family? This part of Scotland is home for me, in a way. My people originated here. I'm trying to trace my ancestors."

"I don't think there are any Beatons in this village."

"My grandmother's name was Buchanan. There was a MacFarlane in the mix, too and maybe some Grahams. It's all a bit vague."

Her entire story sounded vague to him. Anybody could make up a few Scottish names. And yet...he could almost imagine her fitting in here. Which made no sense at all. An American finding her place in an old Scots village? Preposterous.

"Are you Mr. Malloch? Mr. Ross Malloch, the laird of these lands?"

"Aye, that I am. What do you want with me?"

"Well, actually, I'm also curious about a dragon."

Ross tensed. "A dragon," he repeated, injecting as much disdain into the word as he could muster.

"Right. Big, scaly, fire-breathing. You know the type. Have any large flying creatures incinerated anyone lately?"

He managed a laugh. "Are you writing a fantasy novel?"

"A book on folk tales, actually. You'd be amazed at how many there are, especially in the British Isles. It's a folklore treasure trove." She paused, looking at Ross as if sizing him up. Or maybe checking him out. "Most of the villages and towns with magical or mystical legends are proud of them. Such stories tend to bring in the tourists."

"We don't encourage tourists here."

"That's the odd thing about this area—there's no Dragon's Inn or Firebreathers pub. No website dedicated to re-telling the old legends. No ballads to commemorate the heroes, assuming there were any. In my experience, that's unusual. Most people are proud of their dragons. Why aren't you?"

"No idea. Maybe this dragon of yours gobbled up all the balladeers, innkeepers, publicans, heroes, and website developers who knew about him, thus preserving his anonymity." He paused. "If the legends don't exist, what are you doing here?"

"The legends do exist. Great stories—very imaginative. Heroic battles, virgin sacrifices, the dragons punished by the gods for their destructiveness. My favorite has the hero driving the dragon from the skies and extinguishing his fires in the sea. But the beast turned into a sea dragon and stole the hero's lover away to a watery lair deep under some island fortress." She looked up at Mallochbirn Keep. "Rather like this place."

This woman was going to be trouble. Perhaps it was true that her forebears were from this area, or she wouldn't know these stories. As far as he knew, they weren't written down anywhere.

"Sounds as if you stopped by the pub for some of our fine single malt before heading over here."

She gave him a big grin. It was all too appealing, and he felt something move inside him. This was all he needed on Midsummer's Eve—an attractive woman stimulating all the passions that he was trying to keep contained.

She lifted a hand to her hair, which was blowing in the brisk wind. The thunderstorm must have moved off, though, since the sky was brighter. It looked as if the sun might even break through. Kate Beaton attempted to knot her thick hair atop her head, but long silky strands kept escaping. Laughing at her futile efforts, she abandoned the attempt, and loosed her glorious hair. Ross imagined it flowing over his bare chest and tangling in his fingers while he fucked her.

Lust rose with a clamoring din. Looking into her eyes he felt his consciousness slide and his awareness deepen. Something that was sleeping stirred. It perked up its head and took a good hard look. He flashed back to the high tower at Mallochbirn where he'd stood on the ancient battlements looking out to sea. Had it been she whom he'd been summoning? Was that why she was here?

For centuries, the Mallochs had been known as the dragons of Mallochbirn, and dragon lore pervaded the region. The original Mallochbirn Dragon had been the traditional flying, fire-breathing variety, but somewhere down the centuries, the creature had been banished from the skies to the seas. By tradition, the sea dragon was bound to the lord. In some versions of the tale, the lord of Mallochbirn actually *was* the creature—half man, half beast, shifting back and forth at unpredictable intervals.

Particularly on Midsummer's Eve.

Family legend held that in every generation, the Laird of the Isle must take a mate, produce an heir, and bind the dragon to its future master. And so it had happened, for too many centuries to count. The direct line of descent had never been broken. If an heir was not lawfully begotten in the marriage bed, the lords of Mallochbirn had never hesitated to legitimize their bastards. Supposedly, the dragon's drive to beget an heir on whichever woman could produce one was far too powerful to resist.

Ross could not deny that for the past few weeks he had been feeling a strong compulsion to find himself a woman for something more than the occasional fuck. And as he looked down at the lovely female standing opposite him, something deep in the heart of him hissed: *This one. I want this one.*

He was oddly transfixed by her mouth. And her scent—it was light, heathery, and incredibly alluring. Once again he felt the beast inside him stir, more insistently now. His muscles hardened to stone and his jaw clenched as he resisted. What he felt was very focused. *She is for me. Take her. I want her.*

She was young—not more than early twenties, he guessed. A bit young for a thirty-year-old reprobate like him.

They tend to come that way. Brides. Young.

Brides?! What the hell was he thinking?

She was continuing to speak: "You'll have to admit, dragon legends make exciting tales. My Gramma Molly used to tell them to me when I was little. It was she who urged me to investigate my roots in Scotland."

Shit. The last thing he needed was some American girl prying into the island's strange history. For her own sake, he had to get rid of her. If the beast inside him got just a little more aroused and interested in this girl, she would be in considerable danger.

She needed to leave. Quickly. Before tonight.

Thinking fast, he said, "You know, silly though this is, there's another island about 50 miles up the coast with an old fortress. I don't remember its name, but I believe the locals associate some sort of dragon nonsense with the place."

"Really? I wonder why I haven't heard about that. You're sure you don't remember what the place is called?"

It was better to deny than to lie, he decided, particularly since you could hardly hide an island and a fortress from Google Maps. "Sorry, I'm no expert on folklore. If you want sea monsters, you should try your luck with Nessie. This is a great time of year for Nessie sightings."

Which was total bullshit. The way she shot him a quick glance from under her thick lashes made him suspect that she knew it. The orange cat also gave him a scornful look as it paced near the causeway, still waiting for the water to disappear.

"Are you sure you won't let me take a quick look around your fortress? The architecture is remarkable." And she gave him an enormous smile.

He almost melted...

All the more reason to chase her off. Now.

"Ms. Beaton. I have tried to be courteous, but now you're wasting my time. You're not welcome here. Kindly turn your car around and get the fuck off my island before I have you arrested."

Her face fell so much that he felt guilty. Shit...what was wrong with him today? Strangers were never welcome. Even strange women who were lovely, luscious, and supremely fuckable.

"I don't want to intrude where I'm unwelcome," she said, giving him a twisted smile. It was almost as if she couldn't help smiling, no matter how she was feeling inside.

He jerked open her car door and held it for her. She tossed her head. "Okay, okay." She sounded resigned as she stepped past him and climbed in. When she brushed by him, his cock reacted as if she had laid her hand upon it.

This was beginning to feel like the longest day of his life. How many hours until sunset? Far too many.

"See ya," she said impishly as she started the vehicle and turned it around.

Not if you know what's good for you, lass.

As she drove slowly back over the wet causeway, he couldn't stop wishing that he had thrust her up against the side of her car, stripped off her clothing, and shoved himself inside her. Crazy. He hadn't felt this way about a woman for far too long.

Why had he let her go?

Chapter Two

Kate wasn't sure what to make of Ross Malloch. Uninformative and dismissive as he had been, there was something intriguing about the guy. Not to mention how hot he had turned out to be. She could picture him on the cover of one of her favorite Scottish romance novels, shirtless, in a kilt with a huge claymore strapped to his back.

He was beautiful. That was the only word, really, that would do justice to the tall, dark-haired man with the vivid blue eyes who had swept her off his bloody island with such casual, born-to-command authority.

He was not handsome—that was too mild a word. Laird Malloch had worn a warrior's face, austere and stern. His hair was unfashionably long, tied back from his honed face with a twist of leather. His mouth had been set at the start of their encounter in a rigid line that gave no hint of a smile. Slowly, as they'd bantered, that mouth had relaxed a bit, and those eyes had warmed and sparkled. She thought she'd sensed the flare of sexual attraction. Briefly, anyway. Before he'd started swearing at her.

Too bad he was so hostile toward outsiders. People in the village were the same. There was none of the friendliness she had encountered elsewhere in Scotland. Here in this weird place out of time she was the stranger, the interloper, the foreigner. They all seethed to be rid of her as quickly as possible.

Especially Ross Malloch. He wanted her gone. She wondered why. And why had he denied that there were legends about dragons associated with this area? There was a dragon carved into the stones of Mallochbirn— did he think she couldn't see it above the battlements?

Even getting something as simple as a cup of tea or coffee in the village seemed impossible. She tried a place that billed itself as an inn, but she was stiffly told they weren't serving. When would they be serving? At lunch time? No, they didn't do lunch. How about supper? Supper was only offered to paying guests who took a room for the night.

Partly because she was restless after her encounter with Malloch, Kate decided to push it. She needed another chance at the superhot Scot. "I'd like to book a room for tonight. What time is supper? I'll be sure to be back."

The innkeeper, a dour middle age woman, replied with a straight face, "We have no rooms available."

Kate cast an ironic glance around the empty common room. "That's odd. I don't see any other guests."

The woman remained stonily silent.

"I am going to try to locate the graves of my great-grandparents and other members of my family today, so I'll be out and about. But I'll return this evening. I would love to be able to count on having accommodations here."

As she had hoped, the mention of her family thawed the woman the tiniest bit. "Your family came from our village?"

"Yes, I think so. I'm trying to trace them. I'm not sure where they are buried."

"Have you tried up at the churchyard? The new vicar is said to be interested in local genealogy. Rev. Lambeth is his name. Rev. John Lambeth."

This was an unexpected piece of luck. "That's wonderful! Will I find him in the church? I'll go speak with him immediately."

"Aye, you should find him next door to the church in the rectory."

"Thank you. And may I count on that room for the night?"

The brief friendliness shut down again. "No, you may not. As I said, we have nothing available tonight. I suggest you speak to the vicar and then be out of town as quickly as possible. Certainly well before sunset."

"Why? What happens at sunset? Do the vampires come out?"

The innkeeper was not amused. "Of course not. But 'tis Midsummer's Eve."

"Is there a village festival of some sort this evening, then?"

The innkeeper looked furtive. She busied herself wiping an invisible bit of dirt off the counter.

Kate cleared her throat. "Whatever the celebration is, I'll be going over to the castle tonight. I have an appointment with the laird."

She watched the innkeeper closely for her reaction to this lie, and she wasn't disappointed. The woman looked horrified. "That's impossible. No one is ever allowed to go there on sacrifice ni— I mean, festival night."

Sacrifice night? Had she just struck folklore gold?

"I know this is a Christian village," she said, "since you've already referred me to Rev. Lambeth. But the summer solstice is still celebrated in lots of cultures. What are the customs here?"

The innkeeper looked relieved, as if a wonderful idea had just occurred to her. "Old customs, yes, that's the way of it. There's a sort of play, you see, like the old mummers' plays. Rev. Lambeth can explain it to you. He's the right man for the job."

That was all she could be persuaded to say about the matter.

* * *

Fifteen minutes later Kate was seated in front of a comfortable hearth with Rev. John Lambeth, who was sipping coffee. He had offered her some, but she'd declined. Lambeth was courteous, but not genial. He gave the impression of a busy man who was beneficently making time for her.

A big orange tabby leapt into the room through an open window and brushed against its master's leg. Lambeth patted him fleetingly, but he also gave his trousers leg a twitch. The cat looked offended. Perhaps the Reverend didn't want cat hair on his clothing.

Kate stretched out a hand, uncertain if the kitty would come to a stranger. She was good with animals, though, and few could resist when she appealed to them. She projected warmth and welcome to the cat, who studied her. She decided to try a careful mental probe. It was something she had learned from Gramma Molly.

She envisioned a shimmering golden thread extending from her to the kitty, letting soothing thoughts flow along it. The cat cocked his head as the mental link was formed. Reassured and compliant, he strolled toward her and leapt up into her lap.

"You can push him down," Rev. Lambeth said. "I do apologize. He's a fine cat, but he sheds dreadfully."

"No need," she said, stroking the silky fur. "I love cats. What's his name?"

"Scrounge."

Indignation flowed through the thread between her and the cat. *Prince*, the animal corrected.

Kate grinned, and rubbed him under his chin. "You're beautiful, Prince," she told him silently.

He flopped down across her lap and began to purr.

Kate's initial approach to Lambeth had been the family history angle. It turned out that he was relatively new to his appointment, so he wasn't helpful in that respect, although he did offer to conduct her on a tour of the churchyard where the old graves were. She accepted with enthusiasm.

Rev. Lambeth led her up the road to the church, which was about a hundred yards distant from the rectory. The church was a charming old stone building that had probably graced the village for centuries, given its Gothic architecture. The churchyard surrounded it on three sides. It was dotted with gravestones and crosses, many of them very old, with their lettering worn away by wind and rain. The churchyard was well kept, though, with its grasses mown and a riot of cheerful flowers blooming.

"I like to do a bit of gardening," Rev. Lambeth explained.

"It's beautiful." Kate stroked the petals of a yellow climbing rose whose blossoms festooned the low wall around the graveyard. "You're the one who cares for the garden?"

"We have a sexton who does most of the upkeep of the church and garden, but I help out whenever I can."

This surprised Kate, since the reverend had seemed fastidious. She would have expected him to be the type of man who didn't care to dig about in the dirt. Rapid judgments of people were never wise, she reminded herself.

Scrounge, or Prince as he preferred to be called, followed them into the churchyard. He strolled around among the graves, his tail high, peering at the old headstones as if he could read them.

"The oldest graves are here, directly to the back of the east end of the church," the reverend told her, leading her to a neat area with thin stone slabs whose lettering was worn away almost to nothing. Although the stones were covered with moss and lichen, the graves were raked and trimmed. "Some of these go back to medieval times. What surnames are you looking for?"

She told him and they poked among the graves. "What's that large tomb in the corner?" she asked, pointing to a grass-covered mound with an iron gate and two mammoth Doric columns on either side of the black-painted iron door.

"That's the Malloch family tomb. It's as old as any of the graves here. The family has been the local elite for centuries."

Compared to the rest of the modest churchyard, the elaborate tomb seemed out of place. And perhaps a bit eerie. She remembered her joke to the innkeeper about vampires arising after sunset. She could almost imagine a couple of pale, deathly creatures emerging from that mound.

"Do they still bury their dead in there?"

"Aye, so I'm told. It's not been opened since I've been here, though. I believe the current laird's father died about a decade ago, and his mother not long afterwards."

Shortly thereafter, Rev. Lambeth informed her that he had to return to the rectory to attend to parish business. She was welcome to continue to explore on her own. The cat stayed with her as she bent over the old graves, trying to make out the names and dates. She found several Buchanans who had been laid to rest near the lairds' tomb. Several of these looked like more recent burials, and she was reminded of what Gramma Molly had told her about her family.

It had been her grandmother who had urged her to come to Mallochbirn. Her much-loved grandmother had lived nearby during all the years of her childhood and provided a warm, wise perspective whenever Kate got into the usual sort of mother-daughter conflicts with her own mum. Gramma Molly, whose birth name had been Buchannan, had been born here. She and her mother had emigrated to the U.S. after the Second World War, when her mother had married an American stationed in Britain. Gramma Molly's father had died in the Blitz, but her American stepfather had raised her as his own.

Gramma Molly had been quite young when she'd left Scotland, and younger still when her parents had left Mallochbirn to go south to London and help with the war effort. She'd admitted that most of the stories and legends she had heard about the area were a little outlandish. Her tales often began with the words, "Once upon a time at Mallochbirn a strange and wondrous thing happened. Of course, I didn't see it with my own eyes, but..."

"I've always wanted to go back to Mallochbirn, but I haven't had the chance yet," her grandmother had told her before Kate had left for her trip. "You go for me, lassie. Take lots of pictures. And if you happen to meet that old sea dragon, give the rascal a big hug for me."

After pulling out her camera and photographing all the Buchannan, Graham and MacFarlane graves she could find, Kate returned to the rectory.

"Did you find your ancestors?" Rev. Lambeth asked.

"I'm not sure. I saw some MacFarlanes, Grahams, and quite a lot of Buchanans. The names are common, though, so it's hard to be certain if any of them are my forebears."

"If you like, I could pull the old baptismal records, which go back for several generations. Would those be at all helpful?"

"They might be, yes. Thank you."

He brought her several dusty volumes and installed her in his living room with a cup of tea. Kate pulled out the family tree she'd downloaded from an online website and set about comparing names and dates.

The cat continued to follow her around. Soon she and Prince were good friends, and he was once again sprawled in her lap.

As the day wore on, Kate noticed that Rev. Lambeth seemed to be getting nervous. He came in to check on her progress every ten minutes or so, and although he was polite, she sensed that he would be more comfortable if she left. She decided to find out why.

"I understand there's to be a festival of some sort in the village this evening?"

"Yes, so they say. I don't know all the details."

"But you will be attending?"

"Well, to tell you the truth, I haven't exactly been invited, but yes, since I live here and since most of the villagers are part of my flock, I think it is my duty to attend."

"I get the feeling that the villagers are mistrustful of outsiders," she said in what she hoped was a neutral tone.

"Indeed they are. I was born here, but my parents moved away when I was an infant. Even so, I felt quite unwelcome when I returned," he confided. "Of course, it's better now that I've come to know my parishioners."

"What sort of festival is it?"

"A lot of pagan nonsense, but a very old tradition, if I understand correctly. I hold the laird responsible. The villagers, many of them, don't know any better. But he's an educated man."

The Ross Malloch she had met had been rough around the edges, but yes, he'd had the manner and address of a well-educated man. "So I'm to understand that Mr. Malloch is participating in this pagan ritual?"

"Well, he controls the sea dragon, you see. So he must be."

Ah hah! Had Gramma Molly been right about the local legends? "The sea dragon?" She tried to keep her delight limited to a note of mild inquiry.

"Yes, well, I know what you're thinking. And you're correct, of course—whatever the creature is, it can't be a sea dragon. Perhaps it's a whale. Or a dolphin. I've never actually seen it myself. I haven't had the opportunity to witness this event previously." His voice dropped. "Some people say that Ross Malloch is a sorcerer, and that he conjures this demon up from hell every year, to celebrate the pagan holidays."

Kate felt a laugh bubbling up inside her, and had to struggle to keep her expression severe. The cat seemed to find the conversation amusing, too.

"I've met Mr. Malloch, and he did not strike me as the sorcerer type," she said mischievously.

Lambeth's eyes went round. "Have you indeed? Well, perhaps you know better than I, but it's difficult to imagine a laird who practices human sacrifice would be regarded as an ordinary chap."

"Human sacrifice? Really, Reverend. Are you seriously accusing the Mallochs, who have held this land for nearly nine hundred years, of human sacrifice?"

"Well," He looked flustered. "It might not be human sacrifice, but 'twould be improper for me to say exactly what it does involve."

Kate leaned forward, putting on her best intimidating stare. Not that she had ever been good at intimidation. "Although everyone in this village seems to be living in an earlier century, may I remind you that this is not the Victorian Age. If there is some sort of orgy going on at the castle, I'd like to hear about it. I might even join in."

Rev. Lambeth drew himself up straight in his chair. "Very well, Miss Beaton, but I did warn you."

She could have sworn there was a hint of glee in his eyes as he intoned: "Once a year, by ancient tradition, on Midsummer's Eve, the villagers select a young woman to satisfy the lusts of the Mallochbirn sea dragon. The chosen girl is bound to a rock at moonrise and abandoned to her fate."

Kate could feel her eyes widen as she listened. Rev. Lambeth nodded as if to say "I told you so." He continued, "as I said, I haven't been back long enough to witness this, but I've been told what happens next. There is a harsh hissing sound, the seas part, and the creature comes out of the deep. Everybody screams and carries on, including the sacrificial victim. The sea dragon comes ashore, seizes the girl, and has his way with her.

"Some say he turns into a man for this part of the ritual, while others insist he remains in dragon form. The girl is never injured. Or at least not seriously. In the morning, she is found safe and sound, in a deep sleep. Although she is hazy about her experience, there is universal agreement among the women who have served the sea dragon's pleasure that he is surprisingly, er, skilled. Some even volunteer to be sacrificed a second time, but that is not permitted."

Kate endeavored to beat down the slight flush that had risen over her skin at his description. Fucked by a sea dragon? There was something deliciously kinky about that. She tried to envision what a sea dragon looked like, but she couldn't quite picture it.

"You say, Rev. Lambeth, that you have never witnessed this spectacle?"

"Tonight will be the first time," he said, with obvious relish.

"Is there any chance the villagers have united to make you the victim of a jest?"

"Think what you like, but it will be time soon, and you'll be able to see for yourself that I'm telling you the truth."

Indeed I will, she thought, glad she'd ignored the laird's instructions to leave. "Why did you accuse Mr. Malloch of being responsible for this sea monster?"

"If you know the history of Mallochbirn, you know that in their more warlike years, the family members were known as the Dragons from the Sea. It is said that the Malloch clan and some of their kin have a mysterious ability to enter the minds of various animals and control them. The ritual is known as 'Malloch's lust.' Perhaps it's a remnant of the old *droit de seigneur* from feudal times?

"No one seems to know whether the lords of Mallochbirn conjure the beast or simply control it, but even the laird himself doesn't deny that he is involved."

"I see." This all fit nicely with the stories she'd heard from Gramma Molly. Although her grandmother hadn't mentioned the sacrificial maiden.

"So, Miss Beaton, what do you think now?"

"I think I need to check it out." With reluctance, Kate informed Prince that her lap would no longer be available. The big cat gracefully leapt down. As he did, he sent her a message:

The sea creature likes you.

She often didn't understand the thoughts of animals, which weren't verbal in the usual sense. They sent her images, sounds and smells, many of which she couldn't clearly perceive. She was probably misinterpreting what the kitty meant. How did it even know any sea creatures? Cats rarely went swimming.

Chapter Three

The villagers were celebrating. Whiskey was being passed around, and there was a good deal of boisterous chatter. Someone played a fiddle and someone else banged on a drum as the villagers performed Scottish dances. People seemed surprised to see Kate among them, but to anyone who asked, she mentioned her grandparents. That seemed to make her acceptable to them. She suspected, though, that the amount of whiskey being consumed was contributing to her warm welcome. In the morning, they might feel differently about her.

She met the young woman who had been chosen in this year's lottery. Effie was her name, and she looked about Kate's age or perhaps a little younger. She was quite a flirt, and the young men were hanging around her, urging her to share her kisses before the sea monster assailed her with its big slobbery tongue.

Effie, who was liberally downing the local brew, retorted, "Legend claims he has a far more talented tongue than any of you lot!"

One of the young men in particular was being extra-solicitous to Effie, bringing her more whiskey and smiling nervously at her. He was ginger-haired and sweet-faced, although quite tall and brawny. Not a bad looking lad, all things considered. He clearly had a crush on Effie, but Kate could see no evidence that his feelings were returned. Effie was flirting with all the men. How must it feel, Kate wondered, to be madly in love with the chosen girl on a night like this?

The whole event was bizarre, she decided. She supposed one of the villager men must don a costume that symbolized the sea dragon. No doubt he would strut around making a spectacle of himself. But would he and Effie really have sex tonight? If so, she hoped it was somebody the young woman liked well enough to have a little fun with. It would be horrible if she were forced to participate.

Kate sipped at the whiskey every time it came around. It was strong. She soon began to feel lightheaded.

As it grew darker, the mood on the beach changed. The lighthearted banter turned raucous and there was a violent edge to it that made her uneasy. The laughter of the women was shrill, and the shouts of the men back and forth to each other were harsh and rough.

"The moon is up," someone yelled. "It's time. Effie! Enough with the drink now, lass, off you go."

Effie squealed, still excited about all the attention she was receiving. "Let's go, lads. Row me out to the island and let me see if this monster's really as good a lover as the other girls claim."

The women pushed her forward, and Effie was surrounded by a pack of men, who all grabbed at her. She struggled playfully and yelled, "Get yer fat hands off me. I'm not that drunk. I can walk to the boat."

Kate noticed that although they stopped manhandling her, they still crowded close. The redheaded boy tried to put his arm around her shoulders as he whispered something to her, but Effie shrugged him off. Some of the others tried to touch her in more intimate places, which only made the girl laugh harder. She was bundled into the rowboat and rowed out a short distance to a tiny island. It was little more than a large rock sticking out of the surf a few yards from shore. The rock had a spit of sand facing seaward, with waves breaking fiercely over some submerged rocks. The men had brought ropes, and they looped them around rocky outcroppings to secure Effie against the rock.

Watching along with the others on the beach, Kate was struck by the weird drama of the scene unfolding before her. When Effie was well and truly tied, her arms raised over her head and her hips and legs tightly bound to the rock, she seemed to realize that she was in a predicament. She began to struggle in earnest against the ropes. She started asking the men to untie her, then begging them to do so.

They laughed at her. The mood grew even darker, and Kate began to feel queasy. Maybe she shouldn't have joined in the festivities tonight. She was a stranger here, and this was all a bit over the top. Several of the men around Effie were touching her hair, her mouth, her breasts, her thighs. They began pulling at her clothing—a pretty dress that the girl had obviously chosen for the occasion. Were they going to strip it off her? This might be difficult, given all the rope they had wound around her.

The young man with the crush on Effie started arguing with several of his fellows, but one of the older men shoved a whiskey bottle at him and pushed him away from the girl. Looking uncertain and anguished, the boy lifted a whiskey bottle and drank deeply. He raised the bottle a second time, and gulped the burning liquid down. Kate felt sorry for him.

She also felt indignation and concern for Effie, but that wasn't all she felt. Unaccountably, as she watched the men crowding around their sacrificial victim, an insidious heat built in the deep recesses of her belly. It moved lower, between her legs. Jeez, she was getting wet. In a crazy way, she envied Effie. How would it feel, she wondered, to be the center of all that male attention?

The taboo, the forbidden had always excited her.

Before the men could strip Effie completely, there arose a sibilant hum. The strange vibration crept in from the sea, rising in volume and intensity. In the distance, the waters seemed to glow. Something was speeding toward them. Kate felt the force of a jumble of powerful emotions—lust, rage, and fury—barreling toward them out of the night.

She stared out to sea with everybody else. Holy shit. What the hell was that? The waters were parting for it, and, as it moved, it left a wake of phosphorescence glimmering on the surface.

There was a stirring in the crowd, a low murmur of sound, and finally shouts and screams.

"He comes! The sea dragon!"

"The monster!"

"The Zrakon is rising from the sea!"

The men pawing Effie leapt away and flung themselves into the boat. They rowed frantically back to shore. As for Effie, she started screaming, her voice rising high and shrill.

Shit! Were they abandoning her out there? The poor girl was obviously terrified. Kate didn't blame her. Whatever that was out in the ocean, it surely wasn't a villager in a crazy costume.

Effie shrieked. Kate could never bear to hear the sound of a fellow creature in pain or fear. Without thinking, she rushed toward the water. It was one thing to play the part of a sacrificial maiden, but something else entirely to *be* one.

Effie, no longer so proud to be the center of the villagers' attention, wasn't a willing participant in the ritual any more. Kate didn't understand what was happening, but it was clear that no one was doing anything to help her. She still couldn't see what the thing in the sea was, but it was heading straight for Effie, and the weird humming sound was getting louder.

She raced to the rowboat. The villagers backed away when they saw her coming. She confronted a group consisting of three of the village's strongest young men. "Come on, we have to get her off that rock. Quickly! Help me!"

The men looked at one another uneasily, but did not move. A couple of them had just come back from the rock, and they didn't look in any mood to return. She looked around for the ginger-haired boy, but didn't see him anywhere.

"'Tis the Zrakon," one of them hissed. "He canna be resisted."

"She chose it," another muttered. "If she tries to take back her choice, the monster will come for us instead."

Kate shook her head vigorously. The Zrakon? The thing even had a name. "Don't be absurd. It's probably a whale or maybe even a giant squid. It can't come ashore, but it might hurt Effie, the way she's bound practically in the water."

In truth, she did not know whether whales would hurt anyone, but what if it was a shark? The sea was too cold for those, wasn't it? Didn't sharks stick to warmer water? She was already splashing into the breakers. One man followed her, only to yell at her, grab her arm and try to hold her back. She jerked away from him, and he didn't follow her any deeper. She didn't need the boat, she realized. Effie's rock was only a short distance away and the water was freezing, but not too deep.

The surf was rough, but she persevered. She dragged herself onto the mini-island before the sea monster, or whatever it was, was able to get there.

Effie was wailing, tears pouring down her flushed cheeks. "I've changed my mind, I've changed my mind. I don't want to be taken by something *that* big!"

Kate spoke softly to her, telling her not to cry, and to hold still while she cut the rope that bound her. But the blade of her Swiss Army Knife was not sharp, and it seemed to take an age to saw through the rope. If only she had one of those huge, nasty dirks like Ross Malloch.

All the while, the creature was surging closer, its angry hiss much louder now as it sped toward the sacrificial rock. She wasn't going to make it, Kate realized. She cast a quick glance over her shoulder. The thing was almost upon them. Dammit! There wasn't enough time!

The rope parted and Effie tore herself free. She leapt down and scrambled back through the thigh-high water toward the villagers. The redheaded lad emerged from the crowd on the beach, staggering from all the whiskey he'd consumed. He rushed into the breakers to help Effie.

As Kate tried to follow, a mighty wave crashed over her, and she stumbled and fell to her knees. The massive shoulders of the sea monster rose out of the water. Standing on reptile legs, he stalked through the surf foaming around the small islet. He opened his mouth and showed his great teeth to the crowd. His roar was like a clap of thunder. As it died away, Kate could hear people moaning. The creature pounded on his chest and roared again.

He turned from the scattering crowd and looked down on Kate, who had managed to stand up again. She was drenched and shivering. Huge eyes glittered like silver as they considered her. One more ground-shaking stride and he was looming over her.

Holy shit. What *was* this thing? This was no ordinary creature—this was something from the pages of myths and legends. He could not possibly exist...and yet, he did.

The beast they called Zrakon was easily 10 feet tall. He seemed to gain height as he stood there, as if to make himself more imposing, more magnificent. His massive tail curved around him and slashed the water, sending spray all over them. She backed up until she felt something hard smash into her spine. The rock.

Oh no. I have become the sacrifice.

Chapter Four

Squinting through her tangled hair, which the wind was whipping around her face, Kate hoped for a miracle. This thing was either a demon from hell or a real-life sea dragon. His head was reptilian, with a high, ridged forehead, a broad, flat snout and a thick-lipped mouth that was hinged like a snake's to open extra-wide. His vertically-slit eyes were enormous.

His neck was long and graceful, thickening into massive shoulders from which emerged two humanoid arms. His paws ended in blunt claws. Tentacles criss-crossed like laces across his breast.

His torso was roughly the shape of a man's from the hips to the shoulders. His massive haunches supported powerful-looking legs and huge webbed feet. His thick tail tapered behind him, ending in a flipper-like fin that curled around his legs. Along his spine were several fins, and folded flat behind his shoulders were two leathery structures that might be vestiges of wings.

Why would sea creatures need wings? Or legs, for
that matter? The legend she had heard from her
Gramma claimed that sea dragons were the descend-
ants of airborne, fire-breathing dragons. After com-
mitting some nameless crime, they had been banished
to the seas where their fires had been extinguished forever.

But it was neither the reptilian legs nor the vestiges
of wings that truly alarmed her. That honor went to
the mammoth appendage protruding from between the
creature's hips. She had seen the phallus of a stallion
once, as he had been ready to mount a mare. This was
larger, thicker, and covered with what appeared to be
coarse, fleshy spikes along its length. Worse, as the
creature stalked her, its cock twitched and grew even
larger. Shit. Surely it hadn't meant to use that thing on
Effie? It would have killed her.

Not on Effie. You spared Effie that torture, you lit-
tle idiot. The monster intends to use it on you.

Kate liked to think of herself as brave and capable
of dealing sensibly with things that would alarm other
women. But never in her life had she faced anything
like this.

She inched away from him, even though she had
nowhere to go. The rock was at her back. The rough
ropes that had bound Effie were dangling there. The
entire island seemed to shake with each step as his
powerful back legs crashed into the sand. He was rear-

ing over her now, smelling of brine, seaweed, and something else that was male and musky. His arms, if they were arms, slammed into the rock on either side of her shoulders, caging her. She could feel the heat of his body, which seemed remarkably warm for something that had just swum in from the freezing northern seas.

Unlike a fish or a whale, the Zrakon had a forward-looking face, with his eyes on either side of his long ridged snout. He was definitely more dragon-like than fish-like. His jaw cracked as he opened it and roared with a sound that shook both the island and her heart.

Please don't let me faint, Kate prayed. She was already lightheaded from the Scotch, and her terror was making her legs feel as if they were about to collapse. If she was about to die, she would prefer to face death standing, with her head held high.

The creature dropped its snout toward her neck and she steeled herself to have her throat ripped out. But it seemed to be sniffing her. Dear God. It crunched closer. She could feel the tip of its huge twitching penis pressing hard against her belly.

She spared a thought for all the guys whose advances she had refused in recent months. For some reason she'd been off men. As she'd laughingly told her friends, her vibrator didn't make a lot of silly demands. Now it seemed absurd that she'd been so celibate lately. Raped by a demon monster? Was this her fate because of all the males she had rejected?

The monster was looking her over with what she would swear was a man's lust. No, it was far more ferocious than that. He swung one of his arms at her and she flinched, sure she was about to be struck and killed. But the claw seized the neckline of her dress and ripped it away in one savage motion. It flung the tatters into the sea and let out a bellow. Shaking, she looked down at herself, expecting to see lacerations on her skin, but there were none. Those demon hands came at her again, wrenching away her bra.

He had fingers, she realized, as she teetered between humiliation and terror. Their movements were deft despite all his drama. The digits touched her breasts with some delicacy, leaving her to wonder if this creature felt women up regularly. They slid down over her flesh, leaving tingles, not wounds. They were rougher in texture than a man's fingers, but they did not injure her. The tip of one blunt claw stroked her nipple. It felt surprisingly good. She gave a little gasp as her nipple turned hard. An erotic charge shot down into her core, and she could feel herself blush. Her heart was still pounding, but not entirely from fear. There was something wildly sensual about this.

The digit moved away, trailing farther down over her belly. When the dragon's hand reached the elastic at the top of her bikini panties, he made another rapid jerk, tearing her fragile panties to shreds and leaving her naked. Then he studied her body with his flat, silver eyes.

Great, she thought. I've been stripped by a sea dragon, and now the damn creature is trying to arouse me. Were the villagers still watching this spectacle? Probably.

Kate forced herself to raise her chin and meet the monster's gaze. A strange look passed between them. She could see his raging lust, but she could swear she saw intelligence there, too. And she seemed to hear Gramma Molly's voice telling her, "You have the gift. You can touch the heart and mind of any creature, if you just learn to believe in yourself."

The sea creature likes you, the cat had told her.

She drew a deep breath and opened her mind. She could link with the primitive brains of other animals, so why not this one?

Maintaining eye contact, she sent a golden thread towards the creature, envisioning it as a tendril of light that approached and joined her mind to his. She felt a jolt of contact. Then, not a thread, but a golden tunnel opened between them—much larger and more vivid than anything she had ever glimpsed when trying to match affinities with pets. As she entered this tunnel, she seemed to fly. The sounds of the waves and the howls of the creature slid into the background as she sensed intelligence, organization, reason, power.

And then, she sensed astonishment. The great tail slapped the water and sent another wave crashing over her. She clung to the rock and bit her lip to keep from screaming as loudly as Effie.

You can touch my mind?

His words weren't spoken, but thought. She could hear the sea dragon's phrase in her own mind. Like telepathy.

Whoa. She hadn't expected it to work. She answered by speaking aloud. "So it seems."

What are you doing here?

She had the impression that the "you" was emphasized, as in why *you* and not that yummy village girl?

"Um, I'm not the sacrifice. I cut her free."

You took her place? Why?

*"*No one else would help her. I didn't intend to take her place. You came before I could flee. *"*

Intentional or not, here you are.

"It's all a big mix-up. I'm really sorry. Maybe you could return some other night?"

She sensed amusement from the monster. *It's Midsummer's Eve. We won't get another one of those for an entire year.*

"A year can pass quickly sometimes."

The creature growled. His huge eyes were flicking over her naked flesh. *I am hungry now!*

Despite the implication that she was about to become Zrakon prey, Kate was aware that this exchange was remarkable. Animals, even large animals, could not form coherent questions or answers. They didn't have sophisticated forms of language. When she bonded with animals, what she chiefly sensed from them was imagery and emotion.

But he—the monster—understood her when she spoke. How was that possible? Was he some sort of supernatural creature? A demon? Was he about to bear her down to hell? She didn't even believe in hell!

Conscious that she might not have too many more moments on this earth, Kate tried to answer him with dignity. "I'm the wrong sort of sacrifice. I'm a traveler and a foreigner. I don't share the customs of your people."

The beast's gigantic head tilted to one side and he seemed to be examining her with some attention. *What is a foreigner doing on a rock in the Highlands on Midsummer's Eve?*

"I'm half Scottish. My grandmother came from this region. Anyway, I'm a guest. Surely you're aware of the ancient laws of hospitality. Even mythical creatures respect them."

Next you're going to tell me that these ancient laws forbid me to fuck you.

She drew a deep breath. "I doubt you'd find me appealing."

You do look skinny. My intention was to ravish a buxom village girl, who would have been whiskey-sloshed and compliant.

"I hardly think Effie wanted to be raped."

Effie, was it? She heard a loud sound that sounded like sea dragon laughter. *She would have enjoyed herself hugely, and had a fine tale to tell her grandchildren. It is most ungracious of you, lass, to interfere with my pleasures.*

Was she hallucinating this? Maybe she was having imaginary fancies as she died. Like "walk into the light," but personally tailored for a woman who was fond of animals and folklore.

One of his huge clawed hands reached out and touched her on the shoulder. His silvery eyes looked speculative. *Are you a virgin?*

If she hadn't been so scared, she would have laughed. "No. If the sacrifice has to be a virgin, I'm afraid you're out of luck."

It is a great misconception that we expect virgins as the sacrifice. A lusty, experienced girl is preferable. His metallic eyes glanced downwards at his own erect phallus. *All human women are virgins to the Zrakon.*

Kate thought it wise not to respond to that understatement. The sea dragon gave a thunderous growl. He reached out again with one of his dragon fingers and ran it over her flesh, from her breasts to the thatch of dark brown hair between her legs. She flinched from his touch, but she was fascinated by it. Once again, it sent pleasurable shivers through her. This is what comes, she thought breathlessly, of being intrigued with the forbidden—you end up contemplating some sort of monster sex!

I want you. But this doesn't feel quite right. The creature sounded puzzled. *It's not enough. You are different. There should be more. Much more.*

More what? She clung to the idea that there was something wrong. "So, you'll let me go?"

No. We're going for a swim.

Kate tried again to retreat. "I'm not a very good swimmer."

I am. The two vertical rows of tentacles that laced down the front of his chest unlaced and opened. *Do what I tell you.*

Kate stared at the iridescent rainbow-colored scales in front of her. His hide was quite beautiful, close up. She sensed that he wanted her to step forward into his briny embrace. "The sea is cold. I'll freeze."

I will cradle you against my chest and belly. You will be warm there.

"I don't really—"

Just above the top two tentacles, you can see a stubby bud. It channels air from my lungs. You must press your face there and take it into your mouth. You will share my air. I can hold my breath under water for a hundred times longer than you can.

"I'm fine right here, thank you."

I'm taking you to the keep.

She frowned. The only keep around here was Mallochbirn Castle. A sudden suspicion seared her. "This has something to do with Ross Malloch, doesn't it? Is he controlling you somehow?"

He growled. *It's complicated.*

"I've been forbidden by your master to visit his castle."

There was another rumble of what she suspected was Zrakon laughter, and then he lunged forward. He had grown tired of the debate.

Kate felt his tentacles close around her, caging her. She expected them to feel cold and slimy, but they were warm and dry. Despite her puny struggles, she was drawn tightly against the giant pectoral muscles of the sea dragon. His muscles rippled against her flesh. He was immensely strong. He was briny, like the sea.

He swung around, and strode back into the surf. One of his reptile hands pressed her face against him, guiding her to the appendage she needed to breathe. It was larger than she'd expected. It barely fit into her mouth.

Keep it in your mouth. Do not attempt to breathe through your nose. Press your face tightly against me and breathe only through the bud. Do you understand?

She nodded her head. Pressed against his chest, she could see nothing. The Zrakon's hand pressed her head to the bud. His other hand settled on her back, monitoring the inward and outward movements of her lungs. He didn't hurt her, but the pressure was firm and unyielding.

She felt him surge as he dived forward and down, and then the waters swallowed them.

Chapter Five

At first, it was terrifying. Most of her senses were cut off—she could not see, smell, or hear anything underwater. Even though she could taste the salty air that was filling her mouth and her lungs, she was still afraid she would breathe in water and drown. She was also afraid he would dive too deep, where the pressure would be too great for her human body to withstand. She could not control the depth, the speed, or the course they were taking. The knowledge that she had no influence on this wild creature was humbling.

How foolish humans were to believe themselves the master of all beasts.

She could feel pressure against her eardrums, but it was not uncomfortable, so he must be keeping them near the surface. Did he understand human physiology? If so, how?

He was going so fast. The water skimmed her body like fire; the tentacles, wet now, cradled her hard

against his chest and abdomen. His body heat trans-
ferred to her, keeping her warm as he had promised,
despite the cold temperature of the Scottish sea.

He was not quite as large as he had seemed at the
sacrificial rock: from the bottoms of his legs to the top
of his head, he was less than twice her height, although
the long tail added length in the water.

Just as she thought the air was beginning to taste
stale, they angled up and broke free of the water. She
felt his lungs exhale, and for an instant, there was
nothing to breathe until he took another deep inhala-
tion. Through the bud, the sweet sea air filled her own
lungs. It felt as if they were flying, and she would have
screamed with a wild combination of fear and delight if
she could have. But his hands remained where they
were, firmly pressed to her head and back, keeping
track of her breathing.

His lungs full, his huge body arched like a dolphin's,
and they were diving again.

On and on they surged, with Kate relaxing as she
felt easier with the breathing. It was a peaceful
world—devoid of light and sound, and requiring nothing from her but passive acceptance. She could not af-
fect this dominion where sea dragons were in their
element. There was nothing for her to do but submit
and allow his power and strength to carry her onward.
He swam, rose, breathed, and dived, in a steady, beautiful rhythm.

She was no longer cold; she felt warm in his arms...er, tentacles. The only uncomfortable aspect to her journey was the size of the breathing bud, which made her jaw ache. She couldn't loosen her lips or she would drown. Not that the Zrakon would have permitted this. One of his webbed paws kept pressing her face tightly against him.

It was to protect her from losing the contact, she knew, but it felt rough, as if he was forcing her to grip him tightly with her mouth in a kind of oral rape. But this did not horrify her. It was all part of the same feeling of complete powerlessness. They were in water, his element, and her life was dependent upon him.

She wondered if he felt pleasure, embracing her like this. What was the bud for? Did sea dragons have young? Was it some sort of nipple? Many men enjoyed having their nipples manipulated. Without analyzing what she was doing, she darted her tongue forward, exploring the center of the bud. Unlike the rest of his rough hide, his underside, where she was held, was not as rough or gnarled, and the breathing bud was made of even softer stuff. It felt silky to her tongue, and it tasted of salt and the sea.

He shuddered as she used her tongue on him, which encouraged her to try it again. At least it kept her mind off wherever they were going and what her fate was likely to be when they got there. She ran the tip of her tongue in a circle once, then again. It felt good on her tongue. She heard a deep sea dragon growl, then heard his voice in her mind again.

Stop playing around or you'll give rise to the Hunger. I won't be responsible for what happens after that.

"What's the Hunger?" she thought back at him. This method of communication exhilarated her.

Trust me, you don't want to know.

"I'm curious. I want to know everything."

Again that rumbling sea dragon chuckle. *You like playing with fire, girl?*

"We're underwater," she sensibly pointed out.

He shifted her slightly, and something huge and hard pressed between her legs. She inhaled more deeply than usual as she realized it must be his ginormous sea dragon cock. It felt as if she was sitting on the blunt end of a log.

There was absolutely no way. None. "I think maybe you should go pick on someone your own size. Like a female sea dragon."

Unfortunately, there aren't any in this world.

"You're claiming they exist in other worlds?" If sarcasm could be expressed telepathically, she was giving it her best shot.

The human part of me is more interested in human females.

"So there is a human part?"

Like I said, it's complicated.

"Do you really rape those village women?"

They volunteer, so I wouldn't call it rape.

"I don't understand how you could penetrate a human woman with that and not kill her in the process."

As you may have noticed, I do have other parts. The tentacle that was holding the lower part of her body curled around her leg and stroked her inner thigh. Another drew its tip down her spine, making her shiver. Wow, it felt good. She moaned, almost losing her tight grip on his breathing bud. He pressed her face harder against him.

Don't get too excited. We're not there yet.

I don't believe this, she said to herself, hoping she was blocking at least some of her thoughts from his hearing. A mythical creature wants to have sex with me, and he's going to make me like it!

Abruptly, the peaceful rhythm slowed and stopped. He rolled over onto his side, bringing her out of the water. His clawed hands no longer pressed upon her, and she felt the tentacles that held her against his body loosen.

Breathe the air, he ordered, pulling her away from the bud. For a moment, she felt dizzy. She was almost afraid to breathe on her own.

A single tentacle wrapped around her waist, and whisked her out of the way as he rolled back onto his belly in the water. He released her into the sea beside him. *Swim.*

Instead, she thrashed. Even though the water was calm, the wake his body produced sent waves over her head. She felt cold now that she was no longer enveloped by the warmth of his body. She felt clumsy in the water, compared to him.

A tentacle shot out and encircled her body, supporting her and keeping her afloat. She clung to it and looked around.

They were still in the dark sea, off shore, but she could see the island and Mallochbirn Castle, albeit from a different direction than she had seen it from the mainland.

"We're still near Mallochbirn Keep. Why did it take us so long to get here?"

I had to swim around to blow off some energy. Be thankful. It was either that or this:

An image filled her mind. Kate understood at once that he was sending it to her. She was lying on her back on the stony strand beside the rock where Effie had been bound. She was naked and slick with ocean spray. Her legs were stretched widely apart and her hips were writhing. Something long and slithery wound around her thighs, slowly approaching her curly mound. It caressed her bare skin, rubbing and sucking at her with the tiny suction cups on its underside. Then it poked between her legs and pushed into her while she twisted and moaned.

"What the hell? What *is* that?"

Don't worry. It's just a fantasy.

He sent her a new mental image—one of his tentacles was snaking over her bare breasts. Her body arched in rhythm to the increasingly fierce thrusts. A third tentacle plundered her mouth. Just as she was about to explode in ecstasy, the appendages retracted and the monster crawled forward and crouched over her. Its huge thorny cock was lining up to penetrate her. Rip her open, rather, since there was absolutely no way....

"Stop it!" she gasped, even though she felt excited by the strange scene.

I did stop it, although I'm damned if I know why. You've really messed up my Midsummer's Eve revels, lass.

"Why do you sound so human?"

I told you I have a human side.

"Is the human side of you cold? This water is freezing. I am not built to withstand such low temperatures. I'll get hypothermia."

You're right. My apologies. He heaved her up into the air and deposited her atop his shoulders. There were more tentacles on his back, but they were much more slender and somewhat shorter than the big ones on his chest. His back was tougher, with harder scales and various knobs and dorsal fins. "Hang on," he said as he began swimming toward the island.

He was too broad to sit astride, so she shifted around, grasping the tentacles—which seemed to cling right back—until she was kneeling on his powerful shoulders. Feeling his tough dorsal scales undulating between her legs and thighs as they moved through the water made her flush and feel a lot warmer. But she was wet and still cold.

"I'm still shivering, Zrak. I wish you hadn't ripped off all my clothes."

Do you want me to cradle you against my chest again? That's probably a lot warmer.

"No, I want to see."

Several warm tentacles curled around her. *Better?*

"Yes." I could get used to this, she thought. It's like tentacle bondage. She blushed at the thought, which she hoped he hadn't heard.

It was too dark to see the island well, but it looked inhospitable from this side—all rocks, stones and crags. He swam toward a mammoth cliff; she could not see a beach or even a place for him to step up out of the sea. *We're going to dive again. How long can you hold your breath?*

"Uh, I don't know. Twenty seconds?"

It'll only take ten. Stretch out more—lie down on me. I'll hold you. Breathe in deeply a couple of times first, to saturate your lungs.

She complied. "Where are we going?"

To my lair.

"Oh." She slid her legs behind her and pressed her torso, carefully, along his back. It was not as comfortable as being pressed to his chest. Various hard protrusions from his armored hide jutted into her. His tentacles tightened on her, holding her in place.

Deep breath, he said, and dived.

He moved fast. They were surfacing again before she started to feel the need for air. The tentacles loosened and she pushed herself upright. They had surfaced in the pool of a small underground cavern. Looking around, she gasped in delight. The walls of the cavern were alight with a multitude of colors— many shades of blue, green, red, yellow and purple. There were huge chunks of crystal everywhere. The crystal light was magnified by small oil lamps hanging at frequent intervals. The light from these shimmered and shivered as it was reflected from one bright crystal surface to the next.

"Oh, my goodness, it's beautiful! Where are we?"

Under Mallochbirn Castle. He lifted and deposited her into shallow, warm water. She found her footing and walked out of the water to a beach of fine white sand. She started to squeeze out her hair, which was loose and heavy with seawater.

The sea dragon swam around in the pool, watching her. She felt the heat of his gaze and sensed that he was holding himself back with remarkable restraint. He wanted to do the things he had shown her. He could barely stop himself from moving ahead with the entire program. But he had restrained himself. He hadn't hurt her. In fact, he'd been remarkably courteous and gentle with her, despite having carried her off to his lair.

You're sexy with your hair down.

"Wouldn't you find me more attractive with big teeth, scales, and tail?"

No. Feel me. Down the golden tunnel rolled an onslaught of his emotions—blustering through her. Fiercest of all was the Hunger. It was more than a man's lust—it was a primal storm of need and desire. Like the light, it seemed to radiate around the cavern, from crystal to crystal, infinitely magnified.

You are mine, Catriona Beaton. I want you, and I will have you. You are in my world now, and you cannot escape your fate.

Kate gasped, more shocked by this than by anything that had happened on this strange, wondrous night. "How do you know my name? He told you, didn't he? Ross Malloch. Or am I dreaming this whole crazy thing? I must be dreaming, but what a dream. I don't think I want to wake up."

Yes, it is a dream. For now, that's all it is. You will not remember this until I give you permission.

Also, you will remain at Mallochbirn. You are mine. You cannot leave. Now lie down in the sand. Lie down and go to sleep.

"But—"

Do not be afraid. I cannot touch you unless you are aware and willing. You're safe here. Sleep.

His voice echoing through the crystal cavern made her feel lightheaded, as if she had consumed too many glasses of champagne. The sand felt warm and soft against her skin. The crystals danced with color. Her eyelids grew heavy, and she knew no more.

Chapter Six

Kate dreamed she was lying naked on a sandy beach. The sun sparkled on the waves. Palm fronds and other lush vegetation gave her shelter from the tropical heat. A soft breeze scented with the aromas of bright colored flowers, fruits and spices drifted over her skin. This, surely, was Paradise.

The noise from the sea did not startle or scare her. Even as it grew, she remained calm and content. Lifting her head, she shaded her eyes with her hand. Yes. He was coming. Her lover. A thrill ran through her body and the tropical heat settled in between her thighs. She could feel the petals of her sex swelling and moistening. He was coming for her at last.

The sea was encroaching on her, too. Where before she had been lying beyond the water line, now the waves tickled her toes as they broke. They rose and broke higher, quickly reaching her knees and her thighs. The water was cool but not too cold. It felt re-freshing.

Soon the waves were lapping at her between her thighs, cresting on the mound of her sex in a way that made her breathe more quickly and churn her hips to meet the teasing lash of the salty water. Beneath her butt, the wet sand collapsed a little, sucking at her as the waves slid back out. It was as if the sea itself were caressing her.

She lay quite still as she heard him splashing in the shallows toward her. Huge and magnificent, the crea-ture of myth shouldered up from the clear green sea. Water sluiced down over his tough, gnarly hide, mak-ing him shine in the sun. She wanted to run her hands over that rough hide, pressing firmly so he could feel her caresses.

The water heaved as he stepped toward her on his giant haunches. He was graceful, even when partially out of his element. He glided forward smoothly. The closer he came, the more upright he stood, and his fea-tures shifted until he was more man than monster.

He grinned at the sight of her lying naked, awaiting him. He released a thunderous roar of approval.

She sighed and spread her thighs. They would have to stretch very far apart for him, she knew, but this did not alarm her. She felt lazy and hazy as he came upon her, his enormous shadow blotting out the sun.

Somewhere in the distance, she heard a pounding like a drum beat. She wasn't sure whether there were indeed drummers present, or if it was just the beating of her blood. She moved her pelvis to the rhythm. The motion added to her building lust.

He was all she could see now—his silvery eyes, his crushing jaws, his seven-fingered hands, his muscular chest and belly, against which she had been protectively cradled. He had tentacles crisscrossing his torso. As she watched, her soul on fire, they uncrossed and slithered over her body. All six of them slid to different spots, where they stroked her burning flesh. She closed her eyes.

You are beautiful, Catriona.

His voice was human, his accent a husky Scots brogue. His body turned human, too. In fact, she realized in that hazy way you notice things in dreams, he looked an awful lot like the smoldering laird, Ross Malloch.

She felt his hands on her breasts. They probed, encircled and swirled. There were suction cups on the inner sides of his digits, which clamped down and pulled away rhythmically, sucking at her. She cried out at the sweet intensity of the stimulation. Her thighs thrashed, causing splashes in the shallow water where she lay. When one of the fingers—or was it a tentacle—touched the lips of her pussy, she screamed. It darted around, moving, exploring, driving her mad with the strangest and wildest pleasure she had ever known.

One member, bigger than its fellows, slipped to the threshold of her vagina. The tip probed her. It slid easily into her hot wetness. It moved sinuously inside her, penetrating more deeply, its thickness increasing. She was not sure if she was arching to the stimulation or if the increasingly thick appendage was lifting her hips from the inside as it writhed deliciously within her.

As her bottom came off the sand, she felt another probe being inserted into her ass, pushing past the muscle there and twisting snake-like in time with its mate in her pussy. Then there was intense suction from the one on her clit. She screamed again in wild abandon, probed and massaged all over.

She was coming violently when the probes withdrew and a huge cock pressed against her pussy. She was open, wet, and ready. She felt a sharp, startling pain beginning in her core as something unbelievably huge tried to force itself inside her. But it seemed to be making headway. It was even starting to feel good...

Kate came awake with her heart pounding, her body sweating, and... Whoa. There were pulses of pleasure reverberating between her thighs. She realized with some amusement that she had just had a vivid erotic dream. She pressed her hand to her mound, which was still throbbing with aftershocks. She groaned. A man-monster with magical fingers? Or had they been tentacles?

She didn't think she'd ever had *that* dream before. It had been pretty damn good though, she admitted, squeezing her thighs together and laughing. Too bad there were no warm waters and shady palm trees on the northwest coast of Scotland!

Wait. She jerked upright to a sitting position. She looked around the unfamiliar room. The sensual aftermath of pleasure fled as she struggled to recall how she had gotten here. And where the hell *here* was.

She was in a warm bed in an old-fashioned bedchamber, tucked up among silky sheets and wool blankets with clan colors. The soft light filtering in the windows from outside told her it was morning. There had been an inn in Mallochbirn village, she remembered. But they'd told her they had no rooms available.

She sat up and pushed the covers down. She was clad in a cotton nightgown that was not her own. Underneath it, she was naked.

As she moved one leg from under the covers, fragments of the dream came back to her. The entirety of it was already fading. She shook her head, confused. Had she dreamed of a man or a sea monster? The images had shifted back and forth between the two forms— mythical then human. Human then mythical.

She blinked, trying to clear her mind. It ought to feel like a nightmare, but it had been delicious. Jeez. She must have drunk too much last night.

She rose and crossed the cold floor of the room on bare feet. Brrr! She reached back for a blanket from the bed and wrapped it around her. It might officially be summer, but this chamber was hardly what she would call warm.

She opened the first door she saw, which led to a small bathroom. Shutting it again, she surveyed the rest of the room. There was a window in the rounded wall. Was she in some kind of tower? She looked out and saw nothing but sea and rocks. She dragged the window open and stuck her head out, craning her neck to extend her perspective. Now she could see the headland and a few buildings belonging to the village. The steeple of the church was visible, just.

She must be on Mallochbirn Isle, in the castle itself. The castle that had supposedly been off limits yesterday.

How had she gotten here? She focused, trying to remember. Never having been a big drinker, Kate had never before woken up in the morning with no memory of how she'd spent the previous night. She hoped she hadn't been drugged. Did they even have date rape drugs in this remote area of Scotland? At least she hadn't awakened naked in bed with some stranger.

She imagined waking naked in bed with the hot Scot. *That* wouldn't be such an awful fate.

He must have brought her here. Ross Malloch.

Now what? Was she some kind of prisoner? She crossed to the other door in the room and tugged at it. It opened into a short corridor with a winding stone stairway leading down. She could leave her room, at least. She remembered Effie, the excited girl who had been waiting for her demon lover to rise from the sea. Such nonsense. Had she missed the entire ceremony? Damn that whiskey! She hoped the girl was okay.

First order, clothes. Kate couldn't recall what she had been wearing last night. But a dress and a sweater that belonged to her were neatly folded on a chest standing at the bottom of her large bedstead. Underwear, too. She shed her blanket and dressed. Her backpack was there. She examined it quickly and found the rest of her things intact.

She dug for her cell phone. There was still some battery power left, but it wasn't picking up a signal. Figures. This part of Scotland seemed to be stuck in a former century.

Ten minutes later, Kate was downstairs, exploring the castle. It must have been renovated at some point, although not entirely. There was a central area that had been brought up to modern standards, but other parts of the keep had been left to rusticate in medieval splendor. She followed her nose to a huge kitchen, where a round-cheeked woman was bending over a gas range stirring a cast-iron pot. Kate stopped on the threshold, enjoying the smell of fresh bread baking. "Hullo? Excuse me for disturbing you."

The woman turned, holding up her wooden spoon, and beamed at her. "Good morning to you, Miss. You needn't have come down. I was going to bring up a tray."

"Oh no, that's not necessary. My name is Kate."

"And I'm Irene Dumfries, dear. I have some water boiling for tea, if that suits you?"

"Yes, please, that would be wonderful."

While the tea was brewing, Kate asked, "Mrs. Dumfries, did you notice what time I got here last night? I must have been celebrating a little too hard in the village last night. I'm afraid I don't remember my arrival."

"Everyone enjoys the festivities on Midsummer's Eve," Mrs. Dumfries said, smiling broadly. "'Tis common to be vague about it in the morning. I didn't see you come in, though. I have to be up to get the bread baking, you see, so I'm always in bed early. Did you take a few too many swallows of our fine whiskey? Never you mind. My cooking will fix you up in no time. How about a nice bowl of oat porridge?"

Fortunately, she liked oats. The grain figured in many of the dishes she had tried in the Highlands.

"Where is the laird? I'd like to have a chat with him this morning."

"The Master ordered that you be brought to his study as soon as you were up and about and finished with breakfast."

She was tempted to chug her tea and bolt. She had a lot of questions for the mysterious Ross Malloch. But the porridge smelled so good that she ate it in a leisurely manner. The Master had ordered her to report to him, had he? Well, he could jolly well wait.

* * *

When Ross heard Kate's voice outside his study door, his body reacted. His dick, which was being damned obstreperous this morning, rose aggressively. He was grateful he hadn't donned tight pants.

She knocked on the wide oaken door. He waited a moment to try to compose himself, and then shouted for her to enter.

Kate did so. She was wearing a light summer dress and a cardigan. They must have been in the pack that he had ordered retrieved from her car. Her car was still in the village at the inn, where he had arranged for parking.

"Good morning," he said.

She approached his desk. She regarded him with her head tilted slightly to one side. "What am I doing here? Did I drink too much or did you drug me? LSD, perhaps? I hear that causes trippy hallucinations."

He had considered blaming the whole thing on hallucinogens. Or even an excess of single malt and a lively imagination. But he'd hoped she wouldn't remember.

He gestured to the chair across from his desk. "Please sit." He had placed the desk between them deliberately. It was a barrier. Without it, he was afraid he might grab her. He might even shift to the sea dragon right here, out of the water. Never had he felt less in control.

"I prefer to stand."

Contrary woman. But he loved her spirit, her courage. He remembered the way she had squared her shoulders and bravely confronted the monster, even though she must have been terrified. No one had ever done that before.

She was his. It seemed impossible, yet it must be true. He had bonded with her mentally. She had not made any attempt to resist his invasion of her deepest and most private self. In fact, she had initiated their mental bond. Her connection with the untamed sea dragon had been powerful. She had violated the annual Midsummer's Eve ritual, and the Zrakon could have killed her for that. Instead, he had gazed upon her in awe.

The hunger that had swept him last night was stronger than anything he had ever experienced. His extra-acute senses had sensed her heartbeat, her breathing, every slight movement she made. He had been inside her mind. He wanted to explore her again, mind, body and soul. He wanted to be inside her in every possible way.

"We need to talk," he said.

"No kidding. I woke up a little while ago in a bedroom where I don't recall going to sleep. I must have drunk too much of that delicious whiskey. I don't remember much about last night. But I do know that the last time we met, you were swearing at me and threatening to have me arrested if I didn't leave your forbidden island."

She had the most pleasant, musical voice. He could listen to her talk all day. Even when she was annoyed with him.

Focus, he ordered himself.

She didn't remember. Thank the gods for that. He hadn't been certain the command to forget would work on her. He didn't understand all the aspects of his magic, which he didn't use often. Never before had he found himself in a predicament like this one.

He couldn't stop staring at her. Even if he'd tried, he didn't think he could have dreamed her up. She was exactly the sort of woman he pictured in some of his most outrageous fantasies. Her hair was such a deep black-brown that it had a sheen, as if complete darkness produced an aura of color. In contrast, her skin was ivory pale and flawless. When she blushed or grew angry, as she had been yesterday morning when he'd ordered her off the isle, rosy pink suffused her cheeks, making her face and throat look like roses over silk. Her eyes were sea green. Even without lipstick, her lips were a deep luscious pink.

And that was just her face. Her body, he knew, was equally alluring. He had held her in his arms, carrying her up the steep castle stairs and putting her to bed as gently as he could, afraid to waken her. But she had slept peacefully despite the ordeal of being abducted by the Zrakon.

"The single malt is local," he said, endeavoring to keep his voice steady. Just looking at her made his cock jerk in his pants. "It's a good deal stronger than any-thing that's sold commercially."

"I'd expect to have one helluva hangover, but I feel pretty good." She sounded cheerful. He had noticed yesterday that she had a pleasant way of interacting with people. She was a genuinely friendly and outgoing person. He couldn't say the same about himself.

"So why did you change your mind? About having me here, I mean?"

He tried a smile. "I couldn't just leave you passed out on the beach."

"So that's where you found me? On the beach?"

He nodded. He meant a different stretch of sand than she remembered, though. At least he hoped she didn't remember anything after she and the villagers had been gathered on the mainland beach, awaiting the arrival of the local monster. "Do you have any recollection of the festivities last night?"

She looked uneasy. "I remember that everybody thought some creature from the sea was going to make one of the townswomen his fuck buddy. And that she appeared to be quite willing—the result, I suppose, of drinking too much of that homegrown brew."

Ross cleared his throat. "You did tell me you were gathering information about local folklore."

"And you told me there wasn't any local folklore."

"Oh aye. But perhaps you can see now why we don't want this legend known. The annual sea monster mating ceremony is the sort of thing that would bring the press down upon us. Television. The international tabloids. It would be all over YouTube in minutes. Every year the villagers take a vote. Never has there been even a single endorsement for revealing our secret to outsiders. That secret has been guarded for centuries."

"Which makes me rather inconvenient, doesn't it? What are you going to do? Slit my throat with that dirk you were brandishing yesterday?"

From deep inside him a roar erupted. "*No!*" Ross felt his body shudder, and for a few seconds he thought he might lose control. Shit, it was getting stronger. *She is mine*, the Zrakon reminded him. *I want her.*

"On the contrary," he gritted out. "If what you told me yesterday about your grandparents is correct, you might not be an outsider. I don't think you'd have been allowed to remain in the village last night if you were, and you certainly wouldn't have slept peacefully here. Crazy though it seems, I believe this place is protected by some sort of magic. It literally doesn't let outlanders in. If they do wander by, it plants in them a strong suggestion to leave."

She frowned as she considered this. "What about the Rev. John Lambeth? He told me he would be witnessing the festival for the first time."

"He was born here. He has lived elsewhere for most of his life, but he is one of us."

"Well, I've lived in Boston, Mass., USA for all of my life and my parents are Americans. It's only my grandmother who came from this corner of Scotland."

The Zrakon has claimed you as his own, and that makes you one of us.

But of course, he couldn't tell her that. Not yet.

"This is the opportunity I've decided to offer you, Ms. Beaton. I kicked you off the island yesterday, and that was rude. I'd like to make up for it by offering you a place to stay while you conduct that research you mentioned. We have a remarkable library here. I will give you the run of the place. Perhaps you will discover more about your family.

"All I ask in return is that you don't speak or write about this to anybody. If you want to tell our story in some heavily disguised way, as fiction, that might be allowed. Perhaps a fantasy novel that's set in some invented world?"

She returned his look with a level green gaze. "That's very generous of you. Thank you." She paused, and then added, "So I'm not a prisoner here, right?"

"Of course not." He smiled reassuringly. "What an absurd idea."

He couldn't tell her the truth, which was that the Zrakon was unlikely ever to let her leave.

Chapter Seven

The Mallochbirn library was a treasure trove. It was full of wonderful volumes from earlier centuries, gilded and bound in leather. Kate was careful when handling the books, wearing the thin gloves Ross had provided so she wouldn't leave oily fingerprints. Most of the books were novels, biographies, histories and poetry. There were many that she suspected were valuable first editions.

A considerable number of books were written in other languages, including French, Italian, Gaelic, German, Latin and Ancient Greek. There were a few in Russian, and several in a language that she presumed, from its script, to be Persian, Arabic, or Ottoman Turkish.

There were account books from the estate and registers of land deeds and rental contracts. Reports from gamekeepers and fisheries, distilleries and lumber mills. Malloch had invited her to examine whatever she wanted, and she took him up on that, although the sheer volume of the material was such that she could only look at a fraction of it.

She found several historical accounts of events in the Mallochbirn lands, including some information about the tenants. There were several references to the Buchanan family, whom she believed to be her ancestors. It appeared that the Buchanans had been living on the estate for many generations. There was even a record of a marriage between a Malloch and a Buchanan back in the nineteenth century. One Catriona Isabel Buchanan had married the laird at the time, Angus Charles Malloch.

That was amusing. Catriona was her own given name. The Napoleonic Age Catriona had probably been her ancestor. If so, she and the current laird were distantly related, sharing some miniscule percentage of their DNA.

Maybe I do indeed belong here, she mused. What a peculiar and fascinating idea.

She felt oddly content. She had fallen in love with the rough, craggy scenery— rolling hills and rugged mountains, wildflowers dotting the landscape, the jagged coastline, the many lochs, the fiercely pounding sea. It called to her. Her spirit seemed to have found its home.

One of the last documents Kate examined before the darkening sky outside told her that it was time to break for supper was the diagram of the castle and its grounds. There were several interesting things about the keep—it had a dungeon, for example. Probably a relic from medieval times. She hoped it wasn't still being used!

There were also references to an underground cavern. When she read about this, she experienced a strange flash of deja vu. A cavern under the castle? Why did that sound familiar to her?

The final castle feature that intrigued her was in the garden—a maze. She loved mazes. It had been built in the late eighteenth century when such things were all the rage. Its hedgerows were intricately laid out. The puzzle was complex. But as she looked at the maze map, she saw the patterns there. She was good at pattern detection. She also had an excellent memory, which she made use of as she memorized the maze and its solution.

A mischievous notion occurred to her, and she pondered how to put it in practice.

* * *

Mrs. Dumfries beamed as she carried a tray of delicious smelling roast leg of lamb into the Mallochbirn Castle dining room. On the friendly cook's advice, Kate had dressed for dinner. She did have one garment suitable for eveningwear. It was a simple black dress made of a knit material that bounced back surprisingly well from being rolled up and tucked into corner of her backpack.

It was flattering too, clinging to her curves and falling a bit short on her long, slim legs. She didn't have a pair of heels in the backpack, but her sandals looked okay with the dress. It was summer, after all.

The dining room was quite elegant, with a huge dining table set with fine china and silver. Large portraits of Scots—probably former lairds of Mallochbirn—dominated each of the walls. There were four places set. Ross stood at the head. He indicated that she should take the seat on his left. A man she hadn't met carried in another tray with streaming vegetables and other side dishes.

"Kate, this is my steward, Hamish," said Ross. "He takes care of all sorts of things around the keep and the estate. Hamish, meet Catriona Beaton, my guest."

Hamish, a wiry middle-aged man with greying black hair and a dour expression, nodded to her. Mrs. Dumfries, all smiles, added, "We don't know what we would do around here without Hamish. He's our rock."

Hamish looked embarrassed and said nothing. Kate smiled at him and held out her hand. "Pleased to meet you." Hamish's grip was firm but quick, as if he didn't want to intrude on her by touching her hand for more than a split second.

"Is this the entire household?" she asked.

"No, there's also Jamie Dumfries, Mrs. Dumfries' son, but he's probably out chatting up the local lasses. He's nineteen," Ross added, as if that explained everything. Which it probably did.

"But he's a good lad," his mum said, smiling beneficently. "There's also Annie, a girl from the village who's here three days a week to help with the cleaning and shopping and such. But she goes home at night."

"And of course, there's Cameron," Ross added. "He's not around much these days, though."

"Who is Cameron?"

"My brother. He spends most of his time in Edinburgh. Or even farther afield."

"I didn't realize you had a brother."

"I have three brothers and a sister. We have a family house in Edinburgh, and those wretches escape to the city as often as possible."

"Cameron is his twin brother, Miss," Mrs. Dumfries chimed in, "They look so much alike that even those of us who have been with the family forever can hardly tell them apart."

Good lord, there were *two* of them? And other siblings as well?

"Twins run in my family," Ross said. "They show up every few generations. My father wasn't a twin, but my grandfather was."

"So you're the oldest brother? And the elder twin? That's why you're the laird?"

"Firstborn child and older twin. By eight minutes, aye. Lucky me." He sounded as if he didn't really consider it lucky at all.

"They're a fine family, Miss," Mrs. Dumfries said. "You should see them making merry when they all get together."

"Holidays are quite a lark around here," Ross agreed.

The food was delicious. Kate complimented Mrs. Dumfries as she tasted all the dishes, and that lady beamed with the praise.

Kate couldn't help stealing glances at Ross Malloch even when she was addressing a comment to one of the others at the table. Everything he did seemed sexy to her—carving the roast, spooning potatoes and spinach, cutting his meat and spearing it with his fork, carrying his fork to his lips. She had to swallow the laughter that kept bubbling up inside her. If it turned her on to watch him eating, just imagine how exciting it would be to touch him, kiss him, lie down beside him...

Even more thrilling, he seemed to be reacting the same way toward her. More often than not, when she glanced at him, he was already looking at her. When their eyes met, sparks flew, and erotic visions danced in her head. Chemistry was present in the room, and all the crazy protons and electrons in her cells seemed to be yearning to bond and exchange atomic bits with his.

Or something. She had never been too good at chemistry.

There was a good deal of friendly chatter at the dining table, inspired by Mrs. Dumfries, who was both affable and inquisitive, and Kate, who was naturally outgoing. Hamish didn't have much to say, but when he did speak, his wit was dry and gentle. Kate liked him. Ross was genial enough, too, although he sometimes seemed a little distant, as if his attention kept wandering.

"So you said I could explore the keep, right?" she asked him. "I found a couple of volumes about your island's history in the library. And I'm fascinated by old castles."

"Aye, but be careful. The family has tried to keep it well-maintained over the years, but it's a huge task. There are areas that need renovation. The main tower is solid and its battlements are safe, but some of the sections along the western wall need reinforcing."

"What about the dungeon? Has that been renovated?"

He gave her a long look, and then grinned. "No. What a good idea. I should look into bringing my dungeon up to contemporary standards."

Did he mean...yes he did! She flushed. The hot Scot was getting hotter every minute.

"I also read something about a cavern under the keep. Is that safe for me to explore?"

His expression darkened as if a light had been switched off. "No. There are some old caves down there somewhere, but they flooded long ago. The passageways through the stone foundations are blocked off. Don't go down there." He seemed to realize that he had spoken sharply. "It's dangerous," he added. "Try to stay above the ground, Ms. Beaton."

"Please call me Kate." She looked around the table, grinning at everyone. "I'm not used to such formality. Please. Just Kate is fine."

"Kate it is," Ross agreed.

They had finished the main course and were waiting for Mrs. Dumfries to bring out the pudding when a young man burst into the dining room. Kate recognized him instantly. He was the same ginger-headed lad who had been mooning over Effie last night. The only one in the village who had seemed concerned about the girl's welfare.

"Sorry to bother you, sir, but Miz Macdonald from the village sent me to tell you Daisy's in labor and squealing and carrying on in great distress. She can't seem to give birth. Could you come and see if there's anything wrong?"

"Of course," said Ross, immediately getting up from the table.

Daisy? Who was Daisy? Did Ross have a woman in the village? A mistress? A pregnant mistress?

"That old sow is getting a bit old for this," he said. "Get my bag from my office, Jamie, and let's see what we can do for her." He smiled at Kate and added, "I hope you'll excuse me for a little while. I need to attend to this. By the way, this is young Jamie Dumfries. Jamie, bid welcome to my guest, Kate Beaton."

Jamie nodded to Kate. Then he looked a bit closer and did a double take. She had wondered if he would recognize her. Apparently he did. She flushed slightly, although she wasn't sure why. She couldn't recall what had happened after Effie had been bound to that rock. She was tempted to ask, but the question seemed inappropriate for the dinner table. So she said, "Who is Daisy?"

"Daisy is a pig, Kate. And I am the local vet."

Ross hurried out, leaving Kate staring after him in surprise. He was a veterinarian? She felt like a fool for not realizing that a modern man must have something more important to do all day than sit in his ancient keep and laird about the place.

A vet. Wow. With her natural empathy for animals, she had once dreamed of being a vet herself, but her lack of aptitude for chemistry, biology and mathematics had scuttled that dream.

Malloch hadn't returned when Kate went to bed that night. She had wanted to wait up for this man, whom she found increasingly fascinating. But a curious lassitude set in after the big dinner. When she went up to her room to change into something more casual, she lay down for a quick nap, and didn't awaken until morning.

Chapter Eight

Three days later, Kate climbed the circular staircase in the castle tower to survey the countryside. It was quite a climb, but the view from the battlements was magnificent. It was a clear day, and the sea pounded against the rocks of the island on three sides. On the fourth side was the causeway to the village.

Mallochbirn Village was a quiet place, even on market days. She had learned that only about 400 people lived there, and even fewer populated the cottages and farms on the rest of the Mallochbirn estate. According to Mrs. Dumfries, many young people of the village left for a few years to pursue their educations and careers in other parts of the country, but some of them eventually returned. "No one loves you like your family and friends," she explained. "Besides, life is good here. Calm. Pleasant. Not stressful the way it is everywhere else in this cruel world."

Kate was inclined to agree. She had felt unusually tranquil. The library was full of fascinating books and documents, and she had already discovered a great deal about her ancestors, the Buchanans and the Grahams. The Mallochbirn library possessed far more interesting documents than the parish record room.

Genealogical records revealed that she was distantly related to several of the other families in the area. She was making a list of the families in the village whom she wanted to visit, in order to compare notes on their histories.

She hadn't actually made any visits, though. Perhaps she should do so today? She recalled that Hamish had told her that her car was parked over at the inn. She ought to go there and start it. She'd rented the car for a week, but she'd only used it for a couple of days, driving up into the Highlands.

She realized that she hadn't left Mallochbirn Isle for three days. That was odd. But why leave? The castle still had some unexplored areas, and besides, the hot Scot was here. She really didn't have the slightest inclination to go anywhere.

Maybe if Ross had to go out on another emergency veterinary call, she would ask if she could accompany him. Daisy the pig had been safely coaxed through her labor. She'd given birth to several fine piglets. Yesterday, when Ross had held his clinic in his office in what had originally been the castle stables, Kate had stopped by to watch. He quickly noted that she was a calming presence around the animals—mostly pets coming in for their shots—so he allowed her to help out. Ross was gentle with the animals, and she could see that they responded well to him. Animals were good judges of people. They all seemed to adore Ross.

In between patients, she and he had chatted amiably. He was easy to talk to—friendly and open. An affable guy, and sexy as hell. He hadn't made any moves on her, but she had pretty much decided that if he did, she was going to say yes. And if he didn't, she would just have to make the first move herself.

Kate was walking down the wide staircase to the ground floor when she met Jamie Dumfries coming up. She and he had only encountered each other at dinner so far, and he was shy around her. She had chatted in her usual friendly manner to him, but he seemed to struggle for words when he tried to reply. On a couple of occasions, he had started to say something to her, and then stopped, looking stricken. Jamie was a handsome guy, with brawny shoulders and the general appearance of someone who could take on the world if he had to. But his diffident manner was at odds with his tall, good looks.

They both reached the broad landing where the staircase swung around at a ninety-degree angle. Kate grinned at him and said, "Hey, Jamie, what's up, dude?"

"Hey," he mumbled, blushing. Kate figured he would flee with his usual haste, but he surprised her by stopping. She stopped too. He cleared his throat and then spoke: "I wanted to thank you."

"For what?"

"For, uh, for helping Effie the other night. You're the only one who did."

Kate's memory of what had happened the other night still hadn't returned to her. She remembered Effie's struggles as she was bound to the rock, and the way her laughter had changed to fear and hysteria. She remembered a strange hissing sound, and a vague sensation of feeling cold and maybe wet. In her dreams, which had continued to be bizarre and erotic, she saw fleeting visions of a fierce sea creature who taught her how to breathe underwater and spoke to her in a man's voice, but the details always faded when she woke up. It was maddening. Every time she seized the memory and tried to wrestle it into consciousness, it melted away.

"I honestly don't remember much of what happened the other night," she told Jamie. "I guess I drank too much of your delicious Scots whiskey."

"So did I. My head wouldn't stop aching for two days afterward. But—" he hesitated "—you're all right? I mean, you didn't, you weren't..." His voice trailed away as once again he began to color. With his red hair and his fair complexion, the blush was all the more obvious.

"I'm fine," she assured him. His embarrassment was catching, and she felt her own face getting hot. She wasn't even sure why. "Are you and Effie seeing each other?"

He looked relieved at the change of subject. "Well, we weren't, you know. I mean, I've had a thing for her forever, but she never even noticed me. But after what happened on Midsummer's Eve, she seems a wee bit more interested." He grinned, looking cheerful. "So thanks for that. We're going to hang out tonight at the pub. So we'll see, won't we?"

"Great news!" She punched him playfully in the arm. His triceps were massive. "You're a sexy guy, Jamie. Don't let her give you any shit. If you want her, let her know she's gotta have some respect for you. At least, that's my advice."

"Ta," he said. "Truth is, I never know what to say to women."

"Ask her about herself. Her interests. Her hopes and dreams. Treat her gently, but don't be afraid to make a move. Most women like a confident man. And just remember, if she won't have you, there're plenty of other girls who will."

"I don't know about that," he laughed. "I can hope, I guess."

As they continued on their separate ways, Kate noticed that Jamie seemed to tread more confidently. Good. She doubted it would turn the lamb into a lion, but maybe there was hope for the lad.

Chapter Nine

That evening was warm for June, and Kate wandered around the garden after dinner. The sky was clear and the moon was nearing full. The garden was in full bloom and the scents from the various flowers were lovely. Hamish had told her that many of the plants were blossoming earlier than usual this season.

As she approached the tall hedges marking the outer boundaries of the maze, she ran into Ross, who rounded the hedgerow from the other direction. They both stopped. She felt that instant pull of attraction that always struck when they encountered one another. He was so tall and commanding. So purely and compellingly male. She could easily imagine him stripped of his casual elegance and clad instead in rough leather and a kilt. The warrior of Mallochbirn, barely civilized and ready to leap into battle.

She wasn't accustomed to men like Ross Malloch. She had never encountered his like. Although he was able to mask his elemental nature with courtesy and fine manners, he could not hide it entirely. In London or Boston or New York, at a party or a club, he would have set the women on fire and the men on edge as he prowled among them, seeking out and marking his prey.

"Lovely evening," she said, giving him a big smile. He always warmed to her smiles.

"Aye, it is that. Taking a turn about the garden?"

Mischievously she said, "I was about to enter the maze."

"Better take a snack. That maze is fiendish. You'll be wandering in there all night."

Since she still had the map of the maze firmly in mind, she countered, "Race you to the center?"

He cocked an eyebrow. "You must have a reckless desire for adventure. Do I look like someone who's likely to get lost in his own maze?"

"All things are possible," she said breezily. "I think I deserve a head start, though, don't you? At least a couple of minutes." As she passed him, she allowed her hand to brush his arm. He gave her a roguish smile. His eyes were merry, his mouth had an agreeable curl to it, and his black hair was shining in the moonlight. And there was something in his aura—or in the aura generated between them—a sensual force that tugged at her. She had felt a hint of it as soon as they'd met, and since then it had built relentlessly.

"You'll probably beat me," she said. "But in the unlikely event that I win, what do I get as a prize?"

"What would you like?"

A thought came to mind, and she voiced it without considering why she was asking. "I want to hear about your sea dragon. The whole story, I mean. And I want to visit that old cavern beneath the castle. I know you said it was unsafe, but perhaps you could accompany me?"

He looked surprised. And somewhat alarmed. "Those old caverns are dangerous, but I'll be happy to tell you about the Zrakon."

"I found an old book in your library that claimed that something in the cavern was the key to the mystery of Mallochbirn." She paused, adding, "You could show me your dungeon on the way."

"I don't actually have a dungeon," he said, but she had caught the flare of desire in his eyes. "I mean, it's just an old chamber, where they used to do god only knows what."

"No whips? No chains? I'm disappointed," she teased.

For a moment, she thought he was going to seize her, kiss her, maybe even throw her down on the ground and sensually assault her. She felt an intently focused desire that sent a bolt of fire down her spine. He leaned a bit toward her, sending another thrill surging through her. It left her brains scrambled and her innards churning, because the thought of his seizing her made her wet.

"Suppose I'm the one who solves the maze puzzle first?" he said. "Would you like to hear what I want?"

"I think I can guess," she laughed.

"I want you. Naked and spread out for me. The heart of the maze would be a nice spot for it. It's grassy, cozy and sheltered."

She could feel her pulse pounding in her throat. *Naked and spread out for me.* Whew! The appeal of losing had just zoomed upward. "I'm not sure I should stake quite so much on a strange maze."

"I think you want to. You're a bit of a risk-taker. I can tell."

"I'll gladly stake a kiss. But more than that? We'll just have to see, won't we?"

"A kiss it is, then. At the very least, lassie."

"*If* you win. Don't get your hopes up. I'm good at mazes."

With that, she darted through the narrow opening in the hedgerows, and set off quickly down one of the paths that opened up before her, hoping she would indeed remember the twists and turns to come. It was dark. She hadn't expected to find her way through at night, and she wondered if she could.

"Two minutes," he called to her. "Then I'm coming in after you."

"You'll never catch me, m'laird. See you in the heart of the maze."

"You're going to regret this, Kate. One minute."

"Hey, no speeding up time!"

"Fine, I won't cheat. But you'll soon be wandering helplessly in there."

"Ha. We shall see."

Ross did not attempt to hurry through the maze. Although it had been years since he had last tried to reach the center, the maze was tricky and he doubted a newcomer would easily solve it. He quickly found that he didn't remember it as well as he thought he did. He followed several frustratingly false trails, one of which led him deep into the maze before dead-ending. He would have become lost were it not for his excellent sense of direction. He was good at this sort of puzzle. Although he could not discern in advance which paths through the maze were false, he could retrace his steps without error and test new paths without becoming confused.

"Are you lost yet?" Kate called. Her voice had a flirtatious lilt that he was coming to love.

"I'm not sure. Are you?"

"I made a wrong turn or two, but I'm making good progress now, I think."

"It's damnably dark."

"Look up. The stars are out, the moon is nearly full, and the night is warm and beautiful."

"Agreed. Did you know that when you're in the maze, sheltered on all sides by the hedgerows, the stars shine more brightly here than anywhere else?"

"I gather that you are very fond of your island."

"I am indeed. But I'm beginning to fear that I might be doomed to wander these hedgy pathways forever."

"Take heart—I will come to your rescue before I allow you to suffer that fate."

He smiled. Nothing was going to prevent him from reaching her.

A few minutes later, he heard her cry out in triumph. "I'm here at last! In the center. I have defeated you, Ross."

He was astonished. How the hell did she do that? Shit! "Seriously? How do you know it's the center?"

"Well, it's round, there's a Pan fountain flowing, and an old stone bench."

"Damn."

She laughed. "Do you need assistance yet?"

"Not likely. It's just a case of eliminating various possibilities."

"You could spend the entire night doing that."

"I would never keep a lady waiting so long."

She laughed.

Now that she was in one place instead of moving through the maze, finding her was an easy matter. He permitted himself the luxury of focusing his senses upon her. It was like unfastening a floodgate—she flowed to him like water, her scents, varied and full of sweet, feminine mysteries; and, even more exciting, her sounds—from the tiny almost imperceptible rustlings of her garments, to the in-out movements of her breath and the slow, steady beating of her blood.

With these perceptions to draw him, it was only a few minutes before he silently rounded the last turn and saw her sitting on the low marble bench in the heart of the maze. Her head was thrown back, and she was gazing at the sky. Moonlight silvered her fine features and made her hair shimmer. She looked almost ethereal—an unearthly creature lurking there.

His lips twisted. He had conquered the maze, hunting her to the heart of it with the single-minded efficiency of the dragon of Mallochbirn, and his blood was up. The urge to swoop down upon her and bend her to his will blazed through his body. It would happen anyway, sooner or later. He would have this woman. She was his.

He made no sound, but her own senses must be acute, since she turned to meet his gaze. She appeared startled, and then she smiled. "Bravo! Still, I did get here first, so you will have to pay your forfeit. I want to hear about the sea dragon whose existence you keep denying."

"You might regret such a wish," he said, sitting down beside her on the bench. He did not touch her, but he could feel her body's warmth. Fearing that such proximity might destroy what little self-control he was able to command, he bobbed up again, and paced back and forth in front of her instead. "But if you insist, I'll tell you a tale of my ancestors and their sacred duties here."

She gave her full-bodied, amiable laugh. "I'm a great admirer of folktales, as you know."

"We do have a dragon. You heard about him in the village the other night. He's called the Zrakon. Would you like to know where he came from?"

"I'd love to."

"It is said that in ancient times this island was a sacred place of pagan veneration and worship."

"And human sacrifice, I suppose?"

"Naturally. Along with wild orgies."

"We mustn't forget those."

"The veil between the worlds is fragile here, and beings like the Zrakon can go back and forth."

"Back and forth to where?"

"To a place of magic and mysticism. At one time, before human memory, there was only one world. All creatures, magical and ordinary, dwelt there. But a cataclysm caused a deep rift in creation, resulting in two separate worlds."

"And magical creatures were consigned to the other realm?"

"Aye. But from earliest times there have been reports of dragons, sea serpents, mermaids, fairies, large predatory birds and other strange creatures in the mountains and seas around Mallochbirn."

"Ah." Her eyes were sparkling.

He paused in front of her. "Deep in the heart of the oldest part of Mallochbirn—that would be the cavern, I suppose—is a place where the barrier between the worlds is thin. The original keep was built to guard this rift. In every generation, the laird must vow to protect the barrier. In return, he is granted some special powers. In due time, after mating and producing children, he turns his sacred responsibility over to his heir."

"What are you supposed to guard this barrier from, exactly?"

"From forbidden incursions. Now that the two worlds have separated, they must be kept apart. There is no magic to speak of in our world. It must be kept out."

"Surely a little magic can be permitted to enter our world. Everybody needs a touch of magic."

He couldn't help himself. He reached out and brushed a silky lock of her hair with his fingertips. "Even a touch of magic can be dangerous."

She blinked, her inky lashes briefly curtaining her eyes. "You're speaking as if magic were real."

"What makes you think it isn't?"

"I wish it were! I'd love to see the fantastic creatures that pass through this barrier. Your sea dragon, in particular."

"That might be arranged." He smiled. "I am, as you know, the current Laird of Mallochbirn."

Her eyes were very bright. "And you have mystical powers."

"So I'm told."

She tilted her head and studied him more closely than she ever had before. With his heightened senses, Ross perceived that she was assessing him on many different levels. He thought he felt a faint brush against his mental walls. He rebuffed it automatically, then wished he hadn't. He knew what it was like to be open to her, and he enjoyed it.

"I would dearly like to meet your Zrakon. Can you summon him through the mystical barrier for me?"

"That might be dangerous."

"Shall we try your powers on something smaller? I hear rustling in the hedgerow there—it's probably a mouse. Can you command its will enough to lure it out of hiding?"

"You like mice?" he asked, eyebrows raised.

"I like every sort of animal."

Her challenge was not entirely casual, he suspected. She had been able to form a link with the Zrakon. The only other person who could do that was his twin, with whom he shared identical DNA.

Ross focused, reaching out with his mind. She was right—there was a mouse nearby. The fact that she could perceive it was telling. Most humans would not have known it was there.

He closed a mental bond with the mouse—a trivial feat, really, and lured it into the open. It scampered obediently toward his boot. He stooped, cupped his hand in the grass, and the mouse crawled into his palm.

Kate, who had been watching him with an arch smile, gasped. She slipped to her knees beside the bench, squinting down at the tiny field mouse that he held out to her. "How did you do that?" There was no skepticism in her voice now. "The poor thing—it's trembling."

"It's frightened." He released the creature, which scurried away, diving into the hedgerow.

"I've never seen anyone do that before. I can communicate with cats and dogs and such. But they don't obey my will."

"I'm not that good with cats. I get along well with most other animals, but cats remain elusive." He grinned. "Rather like human females."

Kate rose to her feet, but her knees were weak. Who was this man? He had just moved them both into a different territory. Ross Malloch had casually done something she would have thought impossible. "How did you do that?"

"I've startled you. Forgive me. I am a vet, as you know. I have an affinity for animals."

"Will you teach me?"

His smile flashed, crinkling his eyes and softening his cheekbones. He moved closer and his voice lowered, spinning a sensual web around her. "Teach you what?"

She felt giddy. She was alone in the heart of a maze with a sorcerer. And unless she was mistaken, he was going to kiss her.

He moved the two paces that brought him close to her. The atmosphere around them thickened. It was as if he walked around with his own cloud of sensuality surrounding him. All he had to do was get near her and she was engulfed, too.

He drew her close. There was heat where his body touched hers. It made her breasts heavy and caused a warm, fluttery feeling in her belly. Desire. She wanted him *so* much.

She felt his fingers brush her scalp, and then graze the side of her throat. He cupped her chin. His blue eyes, intense now, gazed down into hers, then blurred as he lowered his face to hers.

He took his time. His mouth stayed poised above hers while the small space between them pulsed and throbbed with expectation. He brought her closer still, tightening the arm around her waist. His other hand slid into her hair. The air sizzled as his lips touched hers.

The mouth that could look so hard and stern at times could kiss like velvet. He tangled his tongue with hers. The skill of that tongue sent bolts of arousal into her breasts and belly. Her arms slid around him and clung. She went up on her tiptoes and rubbed herself against him. She could feel him along the entire length of her, hard bone and firm sinew pressing aggressively into her softer flesh.

He sighed with pleasure. She could feel his heart thundering against her breasts, and between her legs she was slick and hungry.

The hand that had been in her hair moved. His fingers descended along her back to her hip, then cupped her butt and squeezed hard before sliding up the groove of her spine, one vertebra at a time.

Kate was damp with need, intoxicated by him. Fiercely, she caressed the smooth, firm muscles of his back. He made a low growling sound of encouragement. "Kate," he murmured. His breathing changed and she felt him tremble. His hands roughened, and his touch felt like fire.

He explored her breasts, pushing fabric aside. Her eyes widened, for, as his fingers drifted over her, they gave off tiny sparkles of light, like phosphorescence on the surface of the sea at night.

He seemed to notice it at the same time she did. His hand stopped moving. "Don't be afraid," he said raggedly. "It's nothing." He drew a deep breath and the sparkles coming from his fingers winked out. Kate blinked at the air where they had been, wondering if intense desire could make people see stars.

Ross seemed to realize how tightly he was holding her. He released her. A look of unease crossed his features. "Am I hurting you?"

Kate shook her head. She wanted to laugh out loud. Who was this man, this mysterious Ross Malloch? She had never met anyone remotely like him. He was special. He gave off *sparks*.

How would it feel to strip off his clothes, and trace her fingers over his glowing skin? Her body yearned to join with his, giving and receiving all varieties of pleasure.

Ross cleared his throat and passed the back of his hand over his damp forehead. "That settles it."

"What *was* that?"

"There is a bond between us. You felt it, too."

"Well, I certainly felt something."

"There's a strange old legend about the Zrakon's Bond—I thought it was a fable, but maybe it's not. You are meant to be with me. To be my mate."

Kate backed up a step. "Your—wait, what do you mean?"

"You know what I mean."

She didn't know what he meant, but what the hell, who cared? The energy emitted by his hands had looked like sparkler fireworks from Fourth of July celebrations. How would they feel against her skin? Taking his hand, she brought it back to her breast.

She felt him tense. "I don't want to hurt you."

Her curiosity was stronger than her fear. She had to know how it felt. "It doesn't hurt."

That wasn't entirely true. As soon as his skin touched her, the sparkles started up again. As she drew his hand inside the neckline of her top, she felt both heat and static. The sensation was odd. It didn't exactly burn, didn't exactly shock, but was something in between—a strong tingling, vibrating feeling. "What does it feel like to you?"

"It feels good," he admitted. "Intense." His eyes looked dreamy. "It's warm and it tingles. It makes your skin feel extra soft and silky. It's as if all the nerves in my fingers have been zapped up to a higher degree of sensitivity."

"That's how it feels to me, too. It's as if your fingers have turned into a human vibrator."

He laughed low in his throat. "Really? Well, in that case..." He slid his glowing hands lower on her breasts, letting the sparkles flicker over her nipples. She groaned and arched her spine, bringing her breasts more fully into contact with his magic. The sensation from sparkles radiated from her nipple down in a line to her clit, which pulsed strongly. Her breath came out in a sigh. "Ross," she said his name like a plea. "It doesn't matter who won the race. If you want to get naked right here in the maze, I won't say no."

Ross felt his pulse go into overdrive. Had she just said yes to him? Sure sounded like it.

He knew now the true tenor of their bond. No sooner had she surrendered to his first kiss than the erotic magic of the Zrakon swept through him. She had been seared upon him, body and soul. It was more than just a sexual attraction, far more. She had imprinted on him. She was his mate.

The Zrakon wanted her, he knew that, but he wasn't the Zrakon—at least, the Zrakon wasn't *all* that he was. The Zrakon's midsummer lust every year was an inconvenience, but he had tolerated it since the first time, when he'd been nineteen. Usually the damn creature left him alone. They didn't even have the same taste in women. The Zrakon liked lassies like, well, like Effie.

But one of the most enduring legends of the isle was that he, the human part of him, would one day feel a mystical bond with a human female and fall in love with her. And now his body was clamoring to seize Kate, march her up to his bedroom, tear off her clothing, and fuck her until they both screamed aloud, sealing the bond between them.

The Zrakon always knows his mate.

Control, damnation, get some control. He forced himself to breathe slowly and evenly.

She was his. He let the images of what he intended flow toward her, envelope her. She felt them; he could tell by the way her lips parted and her breathing grew shallow and fast. He could arouse her without even touching her. They shared a telepathic link. That was exactly the way it should be between them now.

He wasn't going to waste this chance, burning hands or no burning hands. As gently as possible, he slipped her top over her head. It got tangled in her long hair, but she laughed and helped him pull it free. He loved her laugh—so deep and throaty. Kate was a woman who really enjoyed life. It was one of the things that drew him to her.

It might be his hands that were glowing with mystical fire, but she was the one whose warmth radiated into all the gloomy corners of Mallochbirn. He was certain that the riot of colorful flowers blooming in the garden today was due to her presence. The entire place was greener and more fertile since the Zrakon had cradled her against his breast and brought her to the keep.

Don't think about that, he warned himself. The Zrakon was growing more and more difficult to suppress. Touching her in his human form, especially when his dick was so hard and heavy with desire, was a dangerous thing to do. The more aroused he got, the closer to the surface the beast rose. Usually the only time of year when it was difficult to keep him buried was on Midsummer's Eve, when he came out and had his fun. But this year his fun had been denied.

Kate had already unsnapped and slipped out of her bra. Christ, her breasts were beautiful. Pert and plump, they were larger than he had imagined. He wondered if, like many women, she worried about them being too large. Why did so many women choose to be so skinny these days? Some of them barely had breasts at all. Kate's were just the right size, though. Lovely breasts, her dark nipples hard with arousal.

He put both his hands on her breasts and let the sparkles stimulate the nipples. At first she flinched slightly, and he knew what she was feeling could not be quite as harmless as she had claimed. But a moment later, she relaxed and even arched into his hands. Her lovely eyes closed and the expression on her face spoke volumes—she was into it. Her head fell back and she writhed like an erotic dancer as the sparkles danced over her flesh.

"It's so amazing," she murmured. "I've never felt anything like it. You're some kind of sorcerer, aren't you? The Sorcerer of Sex."

He laughed, not feeling much like a sorcerer, but wishing he knew more magic, if magic would please her. Keeping one hand at her breast, he slowly moved the other down over her belly. Her skin felt so smooth. Every touch of it reverberated in his cock, which was just about splitting his trousers. He traced his hand in a circle across her abs, which were well-defined. She was really fit.

She was wearing one of those skirts that clung to the hips rather than the waist, but it was getting in the way. He searched for its fastenings, and she obliged by unbuttoning something in the back and pushing it down over her hips. Then she kicked out of it and slid her bikini panties down her long, lovely legs. She didn't seem at all shy to be naked, which didn't surprise him. He reminded himself that he had already seen her bare body thru his Zrakon eyes. And then again as a human when he carried her from the cavern to her bedroom in the Tower. But even so, her body was a revelation to him.

She was perfect. Her hips were lush and her ass was delightfully rounded. Between her thighs, her dark thatch of hair was full and a delicious contrast to her rose-ivory skin. "You're a goddess."

She laughed lustily. "You're the mystical being here, not me. And you're wearing too many clothes."

He hurried to repair that oversight. Oddly, the glowing of his hands died out when he touched his own body, so he couldn't tell what it felt like to press the sparkles to his own skin. Probably just as well—he wasn't much for pain, even during sex, although he couldn't deny that he enjoyed dealing it out if such was a woman's desire. He would happily spank a juicy bottom or pinch an erect nipple just to feel his partner react to the intense stimulus. If the sparkles excited Kate, even if they hurt her a little bit, his cock—and the fierce Zrakon inside him—would be all the more aroused and pleased.

There was a cruel side to the Zrakon, he knew. If the beast was out of control, he could be sadistic. Perhaps it was just his nature, or perhaps the violence of his pleasures wouldn't seem so dramatic if his partner was a female sea dragon, with a tough hide. What the Zrakon wanted was not so different from what Ross, the man wanted—to thrust his aching cock inside his female partner. Too bad there were no female sea dragons in the waters around this island—life would be much simpler for everybody if the poor dragon had not been placed under a curse.

"You're too slow," she laughed, and helped him with his trousers. Her hand found him quickly as he slid pants and underwear down. "You're not glowing here," she noted. She stroked him up and down his erect cock, and then she dropped to her knees. The realization that she was going to take him in her mouth nearly made him come on the spot. A moment later her tongue flicked around the rim before sucking him into her hot, silky mouth. God!

She pulled back, taking him in one hand. She pumped her fist up and down his shaft, and then held him still while she explored the head with her tongue. While teasing the slit with the extreme tip of her tongue, she caressed his balls with her clever fingers. Then she drew him part way into her mouth again and sucked hard.

He nearly exploded. He held back because it felt so damn good. He didn't want it to end. There were too many things he wanted to do to her, this bare beautiful goddess who was kneeling, naked, at his feet. His hands dove into her thick hair and pulled her to him as he thrust deeper. He was so hot for her that he knew he was right on the verge of getting rough. He was afraid he would choke her with his thick cock, but she managed to take him without faltering, her mouth a deep well for a thirsty man.

He'd been dreaming about this. Imagining how it would be. But it was so much sweeter.

Her tongue kept working him while one of her hands massaged his balls. The other went around to grab his ass and urge him to take her harder, faster. She sucked him deeper, taking all of him, bobbing her lovely head up and down. One of her fingers found the spot between his ball sack and his arsehole and pressed. Ah, the bliss of it. He was sure he must be hurting her as he pumped his hips into her face, fast, fiercely, driving just as deep as it was possible to go, and groaning as she sucked him into mindlessness.

He was going to come in her mouth. He couldn't stop it. He hoped to hell she wouldn't mind because he was beyond control, beyond thought, burning up with passion. "Catriona," he moaned, reveling in her mouth, her breasts, her beautiful hair. She must have pressed that tender spot again behind his balls because pleasure and muscle tension both erupted together, sending waves of ecstatic release crashing through him. He shot into her mouth, and she swallowed him down, continuing the gentle licking and sucking afterwards, soothing him as he gradually descended.

When she backed off and looked up at him, her green eyes were smiling. "I think we put out your fires, at least for a little while."

Laughing, he sank down in the grass beside her. "That was amazing. Sorry to lose myself so completely, but you sent me right over the edge. You're so fucking sexy." He ran his hands, which, indeed, had stopped glowing, over her breasts. Her nipples were rosy beads, erect and sensitive in the moonlight. "I'll make it up to you, though."

"You'd better," she teased him.

He could still feel the pleasure coursing through him, but curiously, his desire had not died away. As he touched her, stroked her, it surged again. His genitals began to fill and ache as if unsatisfied. It was the Zrakon who was unsatisfied. The beast inside him wanted more than human-to-human congress; it wanted Kate spread out beneath his dragon body, writhing in pain as he speared into her with his monstrous spiked cock. He wasn't sure why his beast wanted that so much, but he felt the rise of timeless ancient lust, and he was afraid for her.

She didn't remember her experience with the Zrakon. Maybe that had been a bad idea—making her forget. She was curious about his sea dragon without realizing that he *was* the monster.

She leaned up to kiss his mouth. He pulled her to him, wrapping her tight in his arms and sealing his lips to hers. It must be the kiss that did it—because his fingers began once again to glow and spark. She shivered as he ran his hands under her hair and down her back.

"The tingling," she whispered.

"Aye. It's coming back. Is it hurting?"

"No. Not exactly. It's strange. Magical, I think. It burns a little, yes, but it's good pain, if that makes any sense."

This time, though, he felt as if he was burning inside. Desire was again overwhelming him, and not just physical desire. His brain felt strange. He couldn't think clearly. He lifted Kate as if she weighed nothing and laid her over the low stone bench, her belly on the bench and her ass in the air. "So sexy," he said, as he spread her thighs and bent to bathe her pussy with his tongue.

She arched and cried out. She was wet and tangy, all woman, delicious and wild. He loved the way she squirmed. He held her down firmly with one sparkling hand on her ass as he licked and sucked her pussy, stabbing his tongue into her.

"Oh, Ross, that's so good," she moaned, twisting beneath his touch.

He inched toward her clit, teasing and circling before sliding his tongue across the firm little bud. She gasped, and he slapped her bottom with his glowing hand, feeling increasingly eager to feel her twitch, hear her cry. She was his now and he could do anything. She was his to play with, his to enjoy, his to torment if such was his need and his desire.

"Is my hand burning you?" he whispered. He sucked hard on her clit. She moaned and ground herself against him. He sucked harder, then bathed the bud with his tongue. "Answer me."

"Um...yes, a little, but it's okay."

He ran his glowing fingers up her spine and felt her jerk and shiver. Over her shoulders and down her sides to her buttocks again. He spanked her lightly. She cried out in what he thought was pleasure, but might have been pain. "Do you like that?"

"Oh god, yes!"

He rubbed more vigorously, fascinated by the way the sparkles danced over the soft curves of her ass. He spanked her harder, and her cries grew louder, more intense. "Shall I use my fiery hand on your clit?"

She bucked and moaned, obviously not sure whether this would drive her mad with bliss or hurt like hell.

He wasn't sure, either, but the dragon inside him didn't care.

"I think I will, lassie." She was his—*his*—and she would know it, now and forever. She would feel what he was doing to her and know. He would claim her with his forbidden fire. He would revel as she screamed out her ecstasy.

But before he could slide his hand into that sweet cleft, she made a sound that he dimly recognized as distress. Beneath the sparkly hand he was pressing against her butt, her skin was a little red.

"It *is* hurting," she gasped. "Maybe a bit too much. It's—"

Shit, he thought, and tore his mystical fingers away. This was supremely hard to do, and as he did it, inside him, the Zrakon roared. He was being denied, *again*, and he was in no mood for denial. The glowing aura was part of his ancient dragonfire, the fire that had been stolen from him and drowned in the sea. He wanted to use it. Now. On her.

No.

The Zrakon's fury erupted. To his horror, Ross saw his glowing hands and arms shimmer and change, turning thicker, stronger, and covered with iridescent scales. The air around them heated and crackled as the change raced up his arms and into his shoulders. Pain and rage shuddered through him. He was *not* going to be denied.

Holy shit. He had never shifted spontaneously before. He had to stop it. She didn't know. The Zrakon wanted her just the way she was—he intended to drive himself into her vulnerable body, so widely spread and waiting for him. Dammit! He had to keep control.

"Kate," his voice sounded hoarse and unnatural. "You aren't safe here. Get up, get out. Kate. I'm serious. Go."

But Kate, languorous from sexual passion, didn't leap up and run away. Of course not. She laughed in her cheery spontaneous way. "Who ever said I wanted to be safe? You're not stopping, are you?"

Fuck. It was like trying to slam the door on a tornado. Any second she was going to roll over or push herself up from the bench, see his half-shifted body, and freak.

If you want her to love you, you great fool of a lummox, he told his monster self, *you'll have to win her with tenderness, not brand her with pain.*

Then he tried to think of the driest possible subject he could imagine, settling on envisioning protein synthesis deep inside a single human cell. Codons. Transcription. Translation. The intricacies of protein folding. Thank the gods for all the years he had spent studying biology and biochemistry, because this utterly confounded the Zrakon. The change stuttered to a halt.

But she wasn't safe yet. His dragon was still raging just beneath the surface. With a monumental effort, Ross held on hard to Kate's spirit. He made her his anchor in the human world, and drove the Zrakon back. Down. Into the depths of him, where he belonged.

A little shakily, he backed away from the woman he and his beast so dearly wanted to fuck. "I don't mean to deprive you, but I think we should wait until this magic attack subsides. Your beautiful butt has a reddish outline of my fingers and palm. Much though I love to see my mark on you, I don't want to burn you. I mean, that could be damned inconvenient later."

He tried to say this lightly, but he was worried. What if he couldn't make love to her in a normal way?

"It does sting a bit," she admitted, pushing herself up and looking down over one shoulder, trying to see her ass.

"We have to get out of the maze. There's magic here, and it's affecting me. Come. Put your clothes on. We can go somewhere a little less fraught with Mallochbirn mysticism."

She pouted a bit, but she obeyed. She kept rubbing her sore ass even after it was covered, but she didn't seem too uncomfortable, and she looked so cute doing it that he felt laughter bubble up. Unfortunately, he couldn't think of a spot less fraught with magic. The dragon would accompany them anywhere he went.

Chapter Ten

Late that night, alone in his bedroom because he didn't trust himself to fall asleep around Kate, Ross telephoned his brother.

"Cam? I need to talk."

"Not now. Call back later," was the curt reply.

"It's important."

"Wait a bit and I'll be with you."

Ross waited, restlessly reliving everything that had happened in the maze. At last he heard Cameron's voice again. "I'm listening. What's the problem?"

They were so much in tune that Cam would have immediately known there was something wrong. "Where exactly are you?" He and Cam tended to respect each other's privacy as much as possible, since being identical twins was intimate enough. But he was curious what Cameron had been up to at this time of night.

Amusement and a slight sense of frustration flowed from Cam to him. "I'm in London at a posh sex club. Would you like a description of exactly what you interrupted?"

Ross grinned. "By all means."

"Too bad. Weep with envy, my brother, and return to your cold lonely bed in Mallochbirn Castle."

"Ha. Might I inquire what sort of sex club?"

Cam swore a colorful oath. "The kinky sort," he admitted.

"I hope you're being careful."

"I'm always careful."

"Sounds like you're dealing with dangerous urges if you're paying for girls aroused by cruelty. If you lose control and shift, you could hurt someone."

"The girls are elite professionals, and some of them even like the work," Cameron growled. "Anyway, I'm not going to lose control. I'm here to gather valuable information, not to indulge myself. It's a client, not me, who's aroused by cruelty. The guy is known to frequent this place, so I'm interviewing a couple of his favorite companions."

Ross laughed. "A likely story."

His brother laughed too. "It happens to be true. You, my blood, are jealous. You're older than I am. Your need to mate is probably stronger than mine."

"We're twins, prick."

"But you're aging faster than I am, stuck on that ancient island."

"It does seem that way, at times," Ross laughed. "But I've just met someone interesting. She's attractive, bright, adventuresome, and a lot of fun to have around."

"That sounds promising. Have you fucked her yet?"

"Not quite. The strange thing is that I can bond with her. Telepathically. The way you and I can sometimes. I think she's the descendant of someone who used to live around here. She might even be distantly related to our family."

"So what's the problem? Do you need my permission?"

"What I need is your advice. A lot of mystical shit is happening between us. And the Zrakon is involved in it all. The compulsion I feel to take her is overpowering. I want to smash into her body and obliterate her will."

Now Cameron laughed. "Come join me in the S&M club. Unleash some of that dark energy here, then go back to your girl and bring her along a little more slowly."

"I can't do that."

"Why not? You know we're different from other men in this. We must release the pent-up energy or we turn into predators more deadly than any we control."

"Don't remind me."

"Sex works. You never get enough of it, living in that isolated castle on your rock."

"I get my share. I just haven't lately."

"Apart from the sex, you could use some ordinary social interaction. Come to Edinburgh for a while. We'll get the whole family together and hang out, have some fun."

"I'd love to, but it's now too late for that solution. Kate imprinted on me earlier this evening. It was like a brand."

There was silence for a moment, then Cameron said, "She *imprinted* on you?"

"Oh aye. It was a volcanic burst of knowledge and recognition and lust, all combined. I knew her for my mate. I wanted to take her immediately—to consummate it on every level. It was torture not to do, you know, everything. But the damn beast was active and I was afraid I'd change. In fact, I started to shift and only barely managed to prevent it. Now I'm lying here in my bedroom giving off steam. My brain is about to explode, and let's not even discuss the condition of my cock."

"I thought that imprinting nonsense was a myth. A myth made up by romantic women."

"So did I, but it happened. It's real."

"I really think you need to get out of that great, looming rock pile more often, Ross."

"I've had other girlfriends, as you know, but I've never felt anything like this. The dragon side of me wants her, and it's not feeling very patient at the moment. Do you think I'm losing it?"

"Shit, man, I don't want to know about this. If this absurd Mallochbirn nonsense can happen to you, does that mean the rest of us are cursed as well?"

Ross laughed, releasing some of his tension. "If we end up in the nuthouse, we'll be quite the attraction—a whole family, skewed in the head."

"Don't fucking scare me. Look, sex may drive men mad, but the insanity is temporary. Even the sea dragon's bond, if there really is such a thing, is self-limiting. Remember our grandfather—no one babbled more about the Zrakon's bond, but he had how many women on the side—a dozen? A score?"

"I think that was after our grandma died. Not that I'm defending the old monster."

"The real question is this: after all the lust has been slaked, will you still want the girl around? After a short acquaintance, how can you even begin to make an estimate about that?"

"I can't, obviously. Nor do I have any reason to believe that she would want to stay with me. She's a prisoner here, in effect. She can't leave."

"Why can't she?"

"I'm sort of holding her captive on the island."

"You can't hold somebody captive. This isn't the Middle Ages."

"Look, I know that, although I'm not sure who is going to stop me. It's not as if she has any relatives nearby. Her family's in the States. Besides, she likes me. Let's just say that things are progressing nicely on that front. Anyway, I think my intentions might be honorable."

"Now that *is* interesting."

"She's intelligent, spirited, and unconventional—she will do quite well."

"Wait just a minute, Twin. You said at the beginning of this conversation that you'd just met the girl. Correct? After all these years alone, you're not going to marry in haste, I hope."

"Tell that to the Zrakon."

"Okay, so why can't she leave?"

"I gave her a post-hypnotic suggestion. I was in sea dragon form at the time. I told her to forget what she had seen and not to go anywhere. She seems to have forgotten, and she hasn't tried to leave. Don't ask me how I did it."

"That's fucked up. You can do mind control now?"

"The Zrakon has grown a lot stronger since Kate showed up. I'm shifting spontaneously."

"Oh aye? You'd better figure this out fast, bro, or both you and your honey might be screwed."

"Thanks a lot. Is that all the advice you have for me?"

"Well, fuck you, here's my advice. Take her. Don't wait, because your lust—and his—will only increase. Give her a few strong measures of that lovely Scotch you have in Mallochbirn and have some yourself while you're at it. It will slow you down. Let her get used to you. After the first couple times, when you're calmer and more in control, focus on her pleasure, and dazzle her with your skill."

"Dazzle her."

"Aye. Do I have to spell it out?"

"Fuck you."

"She's your imprinted mate. She may fight you, but she can't resist you for long. Do whatever it takes. The sooner she gets used to you, the better."

Ross knew it. His mind and his body were both singing with that knowledge. "Thanks, Cam."

"You're welcome. Now may I please return to my, er, mission?"

Ross laughed. "Have fun."

"Good luck with your lady. And remember, whatever it takes."

Chapter Eleven

Kate was dreaming once again of silky seas and tentacles. Many tentacles, large and muscular. They reminded her of cocks, but they were infinitely more flexible. The ways they could turn, twist, curl, even double up upon themselves were amazing. They could suck, too, with different pressures from gentle to brutally intense.

One wound itself around her chest, pinning her arms to her sides. Another lifted her off her feet while a third lashed her butt like a whip. A fourth stimulated her breasts, exciting her so much that she was pleading as yet another snaked up her bare thigh and fed itself into her dripping pussy. It was so damn hot. So damn thick. She moaned and rocked and bucked, but she couldn't seem to reach a climax. She needed something else, something more. Dear god, she was so damn *hungry*.

She woke up suddenly, aroused and unsatisfied, her skin damp and an ache in her core. No orgasm in the maze, she remembered...Ross had been eager to please her but he hadn't been able to stop that mystical glowing.

Tentacles again. This time she didn't even think they'd been attached to anything, but they sure were erotic. Was *that* what the Zrakon did to those girls on Midsummer's Eve? There was no way they could report it later as a pleasant experience if he had actually thrust into them with his monster penis. That would have killed the poor girls. No, he must be all about the tentacles. Maybe that's why the girls refused to talk about their experiences, other than to declare the Zrakon the superman of lovers? Admitting to the tentacle thing would be embarrassing.

Kate tried to bring her thoughts back to hard reality. In the maze with Ross, she had been making love to a man, not a mythical creature. Except....as she lay there in her lonely bed, she felt reality slipping away from her again. Never before had she met a human whose fingers emitted sparks when he was aroused. And despite her own yearning for sexual satisfaction, there had been something a little frightening about him towards the end of their encounter. It had felt as if he was treading right on the line that separated sex from violence. His burning touch had hurt her, but the pain had felt like good pain. Until it had suddenly grown too intense.

But she had nothing to blame him for or accuse him of. She had been willing to take things even further. She'd wanted the torment he had begun to inflict.

Maybe I just like living on the edge, she thought, laughing at herself.

Ross was an enigma. As laird and as the local vet, he was kind, genial, friendly. Yes, he made it clear that he was in charge around here, but the hand that held the reins was not a harsh one. Mrs. Dumfries, Hamish, and Jamie, who all worked for him, adored him. The people who brought their pets to him for care liked and respected him. And except for her initial meeting with him, when he had scolded her for trespassing and ordered her off his land, Ross had been unstintingly courteous and friendly.

She liked him. She found him attractive. Fascinating. Searingly hot.

Damn. Now she was restless. That lustful ache in her core wasn't going away any time soon.

She closed her eyes and tried to sleep again. Run that dream by me again, she thought, smiling as she settled more comfortably into the downy mattress.

* * *

In his own bedchamber, Ross was awake and sweating, too, but from a far more ominous cause. He had been jolted out of sleep, overcome with the type of fiery lust that always consumed him at this time of year. In other years, though, he had satisfied it with the ritual and the monster had gone back to sleep for another twelve months. This year the Zrakon was roaring because he hadn't been permitted his annual grope fest with whichever one of the village girls had won the lottery.

The sea dragon was pissed. He was not going to go quietly back down to the depths of Ross's consciousness, or wherever the hell he dwelt for the other months of the year. Especially now, with Kate so near. Kate, whom the Zrakon had marked as his lover and his plaything. She was his destined partner, and he needed to mate with her. Really mate. As in stick that gigantic cock between her thighs and fuck her brutally.

Christ. Ross's own cock turned steel hard at the thought. He could easily find his way to Kate's bedroom in the dark. It would take but a minute or two to reach her. Even if she had locked her bedchamber door, he had all the keys.

He saw it in his mind, the whole thing. He saw it in his mind: Kate's soft, silken skin. Her dark hair, rich and warm and curtaining her body in luxuriant waves. Her mouth, tasty as a mango, juicy as a peach. Her cunt, juicier still, and hot and tight. Her smile, both merry and mischievous. Her spirit of adventure, her obvious love of everything life had to offer.

Even if what life offered her was a monster.

She was special. He'd never met a woman like her. No wonder the Zrakon had claimed her for his own.

Dammit. His fucking balls were aching and his dick so hard that even the brush of his t-shirt against the head of his cock felt like fire. He needed to cool himself, thrust himself into moistness, feel the smooth walls of her pussy gripping him tightly as he ripped into her with tentacles and his gnarled and thorny cock.

He felt something crack and split apart and terror swept over him for a moment before it was banished by something even stronger. The Hunger. Fuck. Once again he was changing, shifting. Head growing monstrous. Skin rippling over with scales. A huge muscular tail sprouting and beating with rage.

It happened swiftly this time. The Zrakon was not about to be lulled into quiescence again with a lecture on molecular biology.

He was going to go to her. Here, in the keep. But if he did so...if he went to her in such a state...he would surely break her. And if he broke her, he would be alone forever.

The last rational thought he had was the memory of Cam's warning:

You'd better figure this out fast, bro, or both you and your honey might be screwed.

Chapter Twelve

Kate had been unable to fall asleep, after all. She'd risen to use the bathroom. She was just climbing back into bed when she heard a loud racket in the hallway outside. Her door burst open with the crack and splinter of wood and a huge, unimaginably bizarre creature thundered into her room.

Even though she cried out in surprise, she knew instantly who he was. The Zrakon. He looked exactly like the creature in her dream.

He stepped closer. "You must come," he said, the words coming out in a strange sibilant tone that sounded anything but human.

He could talk? Somehow she knew that, too. Not only could he talk, but he could also reach her mind. She wasn't even sure whether his voice was being conveyed through the air or inside her head.

"Come where?" She tried to keep her own voice firm and steady.

"I am the Zrakon. I am your mate."

He sounded a bit like Ross, who had also declared himself to be her mate. What was going on? Maybe she was still dreaming? "I am human," she countered. "I can't be your mate. Aren't you supposed to be in the water?"

To her, it seemed like a reasonable question, but the creature roared his disapproval. Kate swallowed, trying to keep it together. This had to be another dream, right?

"He is trying to take you from me."

"Who is?"

"He is!" The words came out in a hiss.

"You mean the laird? Ross?"

"Aye, him. He made you forget. He doesn't want you to know that you are already mine." The creature shimmered the way Ross had done earlier in the night when the aura around him had spread and enveloped him like a flame. "Look at me. Look closely. Look."

His enormous bulk compressed before her eyes. His long neck shortened and his legs straightened and grew slender. Heat poured off him and he began to glow. Kate shrank back against the headboard of the bed, unsure what she was witnessing. She heard groans and cracking sounds. His long tail shrank away to nothing as he shifted his physical form. His scales became flesh. He turned into a man.

And the man he turned into was Ross.

Kate yelped. What the fuck? And yet, somehow she knew it. Somewhere deep inside the transformation made sense. That must have been what had happened in the maze. That heat, that crackling sound. Ross had started to change. But that meant—God, she couldn't fathom what it meant.

Staring wildly at him, she sprang from the bed and made a mad dash for the bathroom door. Maybe she could lock herself in there? But the creature—the human creature—gusted like fire across the room and was there before her, his back against the door. He looked like Ross, but he moved like the magical thing he was.

He was hindering her escape, so she attacked him with fists flying. She seized a lamp from the top of the bureau and cracked it against his head. Totally stupid thing to do. The lamp smashed, but his head took no damage that she could see. She knew it was crazy to fight him, but she felt trapped and confused and she couldn't help herself. She completely lost it. She whirled and kicked and screamed as she did battle. But she couldn't seem to touch him. He had that glowing, sparkling aura all around him now, like a shield, and every time she encountered it, she felt heat and static and saw jewel-like sparks. She could not touch him as Ross. The creature was preventing it.

"Kate, stop. Calm the fuck down. Please."

"Get away from me!"

He opened the golden tunnel into her mind. She felt it happening; she threw up her mental walls. He glided past them even more easily than he had the first time.

Catriona. Kate. It's me. It's Ross. The Zrakon is bound to the Malloch heir when his father dies. It has happened that way for centuries. But it's still me.

She tried to shove him out, but he hung on.

I need you. The Hunger is indescribable, and it's getting worse. You must submit.

He not only looked like Ross, he sounded like him. People had an individual voice, and whether it was transmitted in sound or in thought, it sounded the same. "Are you truly Ross?"

Aye, truly I am.

"Why is this happening? Why can't you touch me?"

I've waited too long, and now I can only touch you in Zrakon form. Last night, in the maze, that was incredible, but it has pushed him over the edge.

"I'm not sure I understand. You're not human? What are you?"

I'm a shape shifter. You know, like a werewolf? I'm the Zrakon and he is me. That is why you can touch both my mind and his. We're the same.

Kate struggled to make sense of this. Like a werewolf? Were they real, too? "So, you and the Zrakon are one being?"

Not exactly, but close enough. Kate. Listen to me. You don't have to be afraid of my Zrakon side. You and he are already friends. I gave you a command on Mid-summer's Eve. I told you to forget everything that happened that night. It was for the best, but there's no longer any point in it.

"What are you talking about?"

Catriona. Remember. Remember it all now.

Kate felt something shift inside her head, and a host of images rolled before her like a film. No, it was far more intense than a film because everything that she saw had happened to her. Time sped up as she relived the events of Midsummer's Eve: on the beach freeing Effie, her encounter with the Zrakon, the strange yet magical swim through the cold Scottish sea, sheltered against the beast's body, wrapped up in his warm tentacles. The mental communication. The intimacy. The sensuality. The sparkling cavern where he had taken her. It must have been *that* cavern—the place of legend that Ross had declared unsafe and off limits.

The Zrakon had taken her to his lair, and then he had made her forget.

Okay, not much freaked her out, but this did. She retreated to the bed and sat down. She pulled her knees up to her chest, wrapping her arms around herself. She had swum with the Zrakon. She had breathed the air from his lungs. His tentacles had been wrapped around her. They had kept her warm in the cold sea.

It had been an amazing experience, but it had been stolen from her.

Something hot and wild uncoiled inside her. Ross had lied to her. Worse, he had controlled her mind.

"You bastard. You stole a whole night of my life. How could you do that? How dare you invade me that way? Where do you get the power to erase part of my experience? Damn you!"

"Kate, I was trying to protect you."

"Protect me? How? By deceiving me? By pretending to be something you're not? Get out of my room. Take your sea dragon and go straight to hell."

He had the grace to look ashamed of himself. But what he said aloud was, 'I can't let you go. I'm sorry. It's too late for that now."

"You lied to me!'

"I was just trying to ease you into it. I mean, I wanted to break it to you slowly."

"Break what to me?"

"You know—the whole mating with the sea dragon thing."

"You can't seriously expect me to have sex with a mythical beast."

"Couldn't you close your eyes and try? It's me on the inside, and that big ugly beast has sensitive feelings. If you would just relax I'm sure I—we—could make it nice for you."

She remembered the erotic dreams. The tentacles. Surely he hadn't...ohmygod, what if they hadn't been dreams? "What else did you make me forget? When you had me down there in your cave, did you do anything to me? Anything I don't remember?"

"No. Kate, no, I promise you."

"I've been having these crazy dreams."

"Even if I were the sort of creep who forces women—and I assure you, I'm not—there are rules to this game, and consent is required. The Zrakon is not allowed to love you without your permission."

"To love me?" She laughed a little wildly. "It's not physically possible. That Zrakon is too big—and there are barbs on his dick. Have you looked at yourself when you're in that form? That's something that no human woman could possibly endure."

"There's a solution to that."

"Really. And what would that be?"

"Maybe the spiny things, uh, retract or something. I don't know. Damn. I have medical journals of all types in my office, but not a single scholarly paper on the sex life of sea dragons."

Her eyes blinked rapidly. "It *is* you, isn't it? This isn't another freaking dream."

It's no dream. You can hear me when I speak to you telepathically.

"Yes, I can hear you. How do you do that, anyway?" She had felt him form the golden tunnel that linked his mind to hers. "You can read my mind. That would be remarkable enough without the shape shifting. Can you do it with everyone?"

"No." He replied in his normal, audible voice. "The only person I've ever been able to do it with is my twin, and even that is sporadic. I was shocked when you connected with me in the surf on Midsummer Night's Eve."

"I've only done it with animals. Never with a human before. Of course, I thought you were an animal. Or rather, a mythical beast." She shook her head. "I still don't believe this, Ross."

"I can't just enter your mind at will. You have to allow it. And I can't read random thoughts, in case you were wondering. You have to direct them toward me, like a conversation. It takes practice."

"So my secret thoughts and emotions are still private? That's good to know! I'm glad there's something that's still my own."

It might not seem so now, but everything you have is still your own. You're still you, Catriona. We just have this odd connection.

"But it's more than that. You and your Zrakon want to use me for some mysterious purpose that has nothing to do with me. So don't attempt to beguile me. And get the fuck out of my head."

In a sudden concentration of pure, raw power, she flung him out.

He must not have liked that, because there was another flash, another crack, and his body bent over and bulked up again. It happened fast. The human Ross melted away and exploded into the giant form of the Zrakon.

His lust must have exploded, too, because he came at her with that huge scary cock thrusting forward as if its only purpose in life were to slake its lust in her flesh. She shrank away from him, sick about her own helplessness in the face of male rage and physical supremacy. The Zrakon was bigger than ever. He filled and dominated the bedchamber. He dwarfed the sturdy old bedstead where she was cowering.

What had happened to the gentlemanly monster who had kept her warm with his body in the freezing Scottish sea? This Zrakon wanted to tear her apart.

Woman. The Zrakon forged the mental link again; it seemed she couldn't keep him out when his energy and determination were so strong. *You must surrender. That is the ritual. The females of this island have served the Zrakon since the world began.*

This is the Way: Go to the cavern where the sacrificial stone is. You and the human will go together. He will bind you to the rock for the sacrifice. He must give you to me. And you must be willing, you must consent. Do you understand?

"I don't consent, dammit!"

If you do not make the offering willingly, I will hunt you down and keep you with me until you agree. There is no way to avoid your destiny. It was written long be-

*fore you were born. You have until the full moon to pre-
pare yourself.*

He whirled, smashed through the doorframe as if it
were made of straw, and stalked out of her room.

Kate stared at the wreckage around her—the
cracked door, the broken lamp, the sea water soaking
into the oriental rug—and, for the first time in years,
she burst out in sobs. After a couple of minutes,
though, the absurdity of it all struck her, and, with
tears still pouring down her cheeks, she began to
laugh.

"Be careful when you return to Mallochbirn,"
Gramma Molly had said to her. "'Tis a lovely, mad, un-
ruly place that will surely set your brain awhirl."

Chapter Thirteen

In the morning, Kate rose, dressed and went straight to Ross Malloch's bedroom, pounding on the door with her fist. She could hardly believe she had fallen back asleep after all the disturbance last night, but she seemed to rest remarkably well here at Mallochbirn. She wondered if that, too, was magic.

As soon as she heard a human voice within groggily ask who was banging on his door, she burst into the room. Ross was sitting up, looking bleary-eyed in his huge bedstead. He was naked. She ordered herself not to admire the sculpted muscles on his chest, and was thankful that he was mostly covered below the waist.

"I want an explanation," she snarled. "Assuming you're going to stay human long enough to give me one. And don't you dare try to tell me I dreamed the whole thing."

He held up a hand. "Please don't come any closer. I'm no longer in control of the shape-shifting."

Her anger felt like a fist clenching inside her. "He—you—told me I couldn't leave the island. That I wouldn't want to leave. Did you put some sort of magical spell on me? Am I a prisoner here?"

"It was more of a suggestion," he said, sounding chastened. "Like a post-hypnotic thing."

"Every time I've thought about leaving, the idea has gone right out of my head."

"You've thought about leaving?"

"Of course. I'm here on vacation. I was going to drive all around the Highlands. I rented a car. Soon the car will be due back at the rental place in Edinburgh or they'll charge me for another week, which I really can't afford."

"I should have thought of that. I can have someone return it for you."

"What if I want to return it myself? What if I want to leave? Are you going to prevent me?"

"No. No, listen. Now that you've remembered everything, I'm sure the compulsion to remain here has been nullified, too. It's just that—"

She stared at him stonily. "What?"

"He is not going to be happy if you try to leave. He—I honestly don't know what he might do."

"You talk about 'he' as though you were two separate beings. Is that what you are? Do you have Multiple Body Disorder?"

"It's difficult to explain. I don't understand it myself. He isn't me, not really. I mean, I never even felt him until I was nineteen. And he's existed for centuries, if the stories are true. Unless he's some strange genetic disorder. As I said, there haven't been any scientific studies done on the phenomenon. I guess, since this shape-shifting ability runs in my family, there must be some bizarre coding in my DNA, but—"

"I don't need a technical explanation. I just need to know if you're going to keep turning into a beast and trying to rape me."

"I'm really sorry about that. I mean, rough sex can be fun at times, but I can understand why you might object to a gigantic snout and tentacles."

She blushed at the reminder about the tentacles, which she didn't find *entirely* objectionable.

"I would rather make love to your human self, but that seems to be impossible, with that aura that lights up around you every time I get too close."

He looked more cheerful. "You would? You'd make love to me?"

She rolled her eyes. Had he forgotten what she'd done with him in the maze? "That was before I found out that you'd lied to me and put a spell on me. Now I just want to leave."

"Kate. Don't leave. Please. We'll figure this thing out. There must be a solution, since the Malloch line has not died out in something like 900 years."

"The male Mallochs haven't died out. How about the women? What happens to them once they are raped by a giant reptile?"

"He's actually a mammal."

Kate was unprepared for the snort of laughter that took hold of her. The sea dragon was a mammal, not a reptile. "He has wings, or vestiges of them. Maybe he's a freaking bird."

Ross began to laugh, too. "I'm a veterinarian. Trust me, he's a mammal." He paused. "I love your laugh. Even when it comes out as a snort."

It was such an unexpected compliment that she grinned at him. "I wish I could say I love your beast's gigantic spiky penis, but the truth is, it terrifies me. You should be a plastic surgeon, not a vet, because I will need a new vagina after the Zrakon is through with me."

"The Malloch women have lived to a fine old age and given birth to other children, so it'll probably be okay."

"You said you had a twin. Other siblings, too. Do they shape shift, too? How many sea monsters do you have in your family?"

Instead of answering directly he said, "Haven't you ever wondered where some of the old tales and legends come from? You told me you were researching folk lore."

"I am, but I've always thought they arose from human imagination. Every kid has monsters in the closet and under the bed. We are fanciful beings."

"Well, I believe there are parallel universes. There are some respectable scientific theories supporting this idea, too. Maybe sometimes there's slippage between worlds, and beings who are supposed to be in one tumble into the other. They aren't monsters in their own world, even if they seem freakish in ours."

"Wait. Are you claiming to have come here from some other world?"

He laughed. "No. I'm just saying that the story I told you in the maze has been in my family for centuries, and, for all I know, it's the truth. There are mysterious beings in this world now, and some have been here for millennia. Where they came from, no one knows. But like humans, they want to survive, and to do that, they have to mate."

"Okay. But let me remind you that there's a requirement that I be willing. That means that you and your monster have to earn my—" she paused, wanting to say "my love," but love seemed like such a sentimental word to use in this situation. They had only known each other for four days. Maybe things had been different in ancient times, but no 21st century couple spoke of love after only four days. "—my cooperation. And at the moment, after discovering that you tricked me, I'm not inclined to give it."

"I'm sorry for that. I—he—we didn't want to scare you. I just wanted some time to get to know you, and for you to get to know me without the bloody Zrakon stomping and roaring and beating his chest."

She pictured the Zrakon doing just that on the night they'd met and couldn't stop herself from smiling. She also remembered, because now she knew what had happened on Midsummer's Eve, that his chest was strong and oddly comfy as he had cradled her against it during their swim. "He is rather melodramatic, isn't he?"

"He likes to show off. If he doesn't start behaving, I swear I'm going to send him on tour in a bloody circus like the freak he is." As he said this, he began to shimmer, and she backed up a couple of steps. His body started to enlarge and heat came pouring off him, driving her farther away.

"Stop that, Zrak," she ordered. "Go back. You'll have your chance, but this is not the time."

The shimmer died away, leaving Ross looking normal. His grin was sheepish. "He's getting more insistent."

"No kidding. What if you lose control entirely? Will you stay a sea dragon forever?"

"I'd better not, dammit. I have a fucking life to live. There are a lot of people dependent on me. Not to mention animals."

"Did any of your ancestors ever lose their human form completely?"

"No. All this drama is over getting the next heir. And having sea dragon sex, which seems to be all the Zrakon is interested in. He might be hundreds of years old, but he acts like a horny teenager."

"So I not only have to fuck a sea dragon, I have to have his kid, too?"

"The child is human. It's not like, you know, giving birth to a monster."

"I am not sure I would classify you strictly as human."

"Maybe not, but if it's true that one of your distant ancestors married one of mine, then you've got a few drops of Zrakon blood in you, too."

That was certainly something to ponder. "When is the full moon?" she asked.

He grimaced. "I looked it up. The moon is full tonight."

Great. Just terrific.

Chapter Fourteen

Kate had prowled the castle like a ghost all day, spending even more time than usual in the library, looking for something, anything, about the Mallochbirn dragon. Hadn't any of the women in the family kept a journal or written letters or recorded their experiences with the male shape-shifters who had lived in the keep for centuries? Damn them. Maybe they'd been illiterate. Why was it only males who'd received a decent education? At least modern society was correcting *that* error.

She was going to have to leave. Or try to leave. She had been compelled to remain on the island, and that, dammit, she couldn't forgive. She was no uneducated maiden from the Dark Ages; she was a contemporary kick-ass chick who was damned if she would allow her freedom to be snatched from her.

Late in the afternoon, Kate packed her things in her backpack and marched down the stairs to the great hall. There was nobody about. Ross was in his office, holding his veterinary clinic, and Mrs. Dumfries was in the kitchen, cooking something that smelled delicious. She had no idea where Hamish and Jamie were. She hoped Ross had the sea dragon under control. She hated to think what kind of panic would ensue if he burst out during one of Ross' examinations of the local dogs and cats.

She felt a little guilty for leaving when there was no one to say farewell to, but she told herself that it was better this way. She like everyone at Mallochbirn. She even liked the Zrakon when he was behaving himself. As for Ross, she didn't even want to admit to herself how much she liked him.

She managed to escape the keep without anybody interfering. The tide was on the way out, so the causeway was high and dry. She felt a little anxious as she set foot on the gravelly path that led to the mainland, but nothing came roaring out of the water to stop her. Half-expecting to be intercepted any moment, she hurried toward the village. She reached the other side uneventfully. Relieved and perhaps a little disappointed, she trudged up the hill toward the village center.

After going to the parking lot behind the inn to check her rental car, which was fine and started up as soon as the key turned, Kate wasn't sure what to do next. She didn't have a plan. Since she really didn't feel like pulling the car out of the lot and driving away, she locked it, keeping her backpack with her. She strolled around the side of the inn to the main street of the town.

The people who were out and about regarded her curiously. Remembering now that the sea dragon—Ross—had stripped her naked on Midsummer's eve didn't exactly make her feel comfortable. Still, she nodded and smiled, and most of them nodded and smiled back, which was more than they'd done on the day she'd arrived.

She debated going back to the graveyard to search for her ancestors, now that her time in the Mallochbirn library had given her more of a clue who they were. She would like to find the headstone of her ancestor who had married one of the Mallochs. Catriona Isabel. But, no. As wife of the laird, she would have been buried in the family tomb, and Kate certainly wasn't going to venture in there.

She passed an open cafe with three umbrella tables outside on the pavement. There was a young couple sitting at one of these, engaged in intense conversation. They were holding hands and gazing into each other's eyes. She realized, with some amusement, that it was Jamie Dumfries and Effie.

Ha! Good for him. The lad had some gumption, after all. Neither of them noticed her—they were too wrapped up in one another. She debated going up to them, but decided not to. She didn't want to interrupt or embarrass them. Instead, she reversed course, heading back down the way she had come.

When she reached the junction of the main street and the high road that led up to the church and the rectory, she encountered Rev. Lambeth hurrying down toward the causeway to the island. He was holding an animal carrier in his hand. From it was issuing loud, anguished cries.

"Good afternoon, Miss Beaton," he said when he recognized her. "Is the laird at the keep?"

"Yes, I believe so. Is that your cat yowling? What's wrong with him?"

"It's Scrounge, yes. He's been restless all day. He won't eat or drink. The desperate cries started a little while ago. I think he's sick."

"And you're taking him to Ross?"

"To the laird, yes. He's a vet."

Kate tried to reach the mind of the kitty, but the animal was too fretful. He was in pain—that much she could tell from the sound of his cries.

"I'll come with you," she heard herself say. She could decide what to do about her rental car later. Besides, now that she knew she could leave the island without a huge sea dragon rising up in her path to prevent her, she wasn't sure she actually wanted to leave.

There's a full moon tonight, she yelled at herself. *If you have any sense, you'll get the fuck away from here.*

But Prince yowled again, sounding truly anguished, and she knew she couldn't go.

Ross was at the door to his office when she and Rev. Lambeth reached the old estate stable area. He smiled warmly at Kate, making her feel guilty. He obviously didn't know she had tried to leave. "Hullo. I was just closing for the day."

"It's an emergency," she told him. "The vicar's cat is sick and in pain."

"Aye, he doesn't sound happy, does he? Come on in then."

Now that he was here, Scrounge...er...Prince objected to being removed from his cat carrier. His hair stood on end and his back arched as Ross tried to coax him onto the examining table. Kate opened the top of the carrier and tried to soothe him while the Reverend stood there looking helpless. "It's okay, he can stay in there if he's more comfortable. Let me listen to his heart."

With his stethoscope in his ears, Ross approached the seething, spitting cat. Prince appeared to be much larger than usual because of the way his hair was standing on end. Kate recalled that Ross had said he wasn't as good with cats, so she did her best to help. "Prince," she crooned softly. "Try to relax. He's not going to hurt you." The cat was dubious about this, but as she continued to talk to him, he grew calmer. Kate assured Prince that he was safe and that the doctor was trying to help him.

"Did he have any sort of accident?" Ross asked the vicar. Between them, he and Kate had managed to get Prince out of his carrier and onto the table.

"No."

"Did he eat anything unusual?" Ross was now able to run gentle hands over the cat's body, searching for injuries or tender spots.

"No. He was acting strange all day. Restless, grooming himself in an odd, jerky manner, refusing his food. A little while ago, while he was sitting in his usual spot on the front windowsill, he began yowling. I tried to pet him, but he just cried all the harder. I decided I'd better bring him to you before you closed for the day."

Ross asked a few more questions, and then said, "I'm not finding any wounds, and his belly is not swollen. Kate, there's a thermometer on the counter—can you hand it to me? I'm going to take his temperature."

Prince was not pleased to have a thermometer in his butt, but he endured it. He seemed a good deal more relaxed now and was tolerating both Ross's handling and her own gentle touch.

Kate thought: I could do this every day. Handle pets with him.

Yes, you could.

She started, unsure where the thought had come from. She narrowed her eyes at Ross, but he seemed absorbed in listening to Prince's heartbeat.

You not go. The cat was looking up at her now, his yellow eyes shining. *You stay.*

"Prince?" she said sharply.

"His name is Scrounge," the clueless reverend said.

"He prefers to be called Prince." To the cat she thought: "You're faking, aren't you?"

The sea creature likes you. So does the man. Want you to stay here with us. The cat began licking his paw, as if nothing was wrong.

"He has no fever," Ross said. "His heartbeat was elevated when you first brought him in here, but it's fine now. I'm not sure what the problem is. I'll draw some blood and order some other tests."

Prince lay down on the examination table and stretched. He began to purr loudly.

"I think he's feeling better," Kate said, amused. She rubbed Prince behind his ears and sent him another thought: "You're one helluva manipulator, aren't you, boy?"

"Perhaps he had a cramp?" the vicar suggested.

Perhaps he saw me leave the keep with my backpack, Kate thought. "How did you get to be friendly with the sea dragon?" she asked the cat in their silent way.

He does nice pats. With his snake-things. Good rubbing.

Good grief—Prince liked the Zrakon's tentacles, too?

Will you stay?

"We'll see. But fake an illness again, my friend, and I'm calling you Scrounge."

A loud purr was the only reply.

After Rev. Lambeth and Prince had left, minus a little of the cat's blood for testing, Kate said, "I don't think you'll find anything wrong with that cat."

"I don't expect to. The wretch did the same thing last fall when the old vicar retired and left the parish. The cat was upset that the people he trusted were abandoning him. Lambeth adopted him. I'm not sure that the good reverend is the best person to care for him, but they seem to have grown accustomed to one another. I suspect Lambeth wasn't devoting as much time to him as the cat expected, so he had a tantrum."

"So you have to be the local animal psychologist as well as the vet?"

Instead of answering, Ross said, "You were communicating with that cat, weren't you? I couldn't overhear it, but I could sense it."

"Well, you did say you weren't very good with cats."

"That's right. And there's a mess of them in the village." He paused. "I could sure use your help around here."

Stay.

"I'll think about it."

There wasn't a lot of time left for thinking, though. The monster had been very clear: she must surrender to him on the night of the full moon.

Ross knew this as well as she did. He was the monster, after all. But he wasn't pressuring her. Much.

Now that she was back on the island, she felt at home. Magic? Ross had insisted that she was no longer under a compulsion. And her will felt free. She could forge her own destiny. She could stay or she could go. What she could not do was have Ross the man without also taking Ross the Zrakon. She thought of the way his gentle hands had soothed the screeching cat. And the tiny mouse he'd coaxed from its hiding place in the hedgerow. She had never met a man with that kind of gift for animals. A gift that exceeded her own. Yet he had a monster inside him.

Maybe that's true of us all, she thought.

The truth was, she was not appalled and disgusted by the Zrakon. He was a fierce and passionate fellow, but he had never hurt her. If all he had wanted was to caress her in various intimate places with his tentacles, she might have happily allowed it. Although she doubted she would have ever confessed it to her friends. No, the problem was anatomical. Despite the myths and legends of this place, human women and male sea dragons were never intended to mate. And yet, it had supposedly happened.

"Ross?"

"Aye, lassie?"

"The Midsummer's Eve festival that happens every year? The one that didn't follow its usual pattern this time? What actually happens between the Zrakon and the chosen woman? I didn't realize this before last night, but you must know. You were there."

"Um, yeah. I've been there ever since my father got himself killed in a skiing accident when I was nineteen."

"So? Does the Zrakon actually stick that Mt. Everest of a penis into a woman's vagina every year?"

He grinned. "You're asking me to kiss and tell?"

"I'm asking for reassurance."

"Okay, well, the truth is, it's always a little vague exactly what happens on Midsummer's Eve. It's a sort of Dionysian orgy. But here's what I think happens— the Zrakon's not stupid. He knows he has an ancient legend to maintain, and he rather enjoys playing his part. Tearing up some unfortunate villager with his hooked dick would not look good on his record. Fortunately, he can achieve a great deal of gratification from the use of his tentacles, which are almost as erogenous as his dick. And the girls seem to like them, too."

"But how does he, you know—"

"How does he come? Well, it seems that if he rubs himself with his own tentacles, it feels pretty damn great. Imagine you had more than one dick and they all were sexually active, and you sorta rubbed them together..."

She began to laugh. "I get it."

He was actually blushing, which made her laugh even harder.

"I told you he's like a big horny teenager. Trust me, he's quite creative about getting himself off."

"So I'm supposed to have sex with a big horny teenager?"

"Don't worry about robbing the cradle. He's centuries older than you."

"That's the least of my worries!" She had a random thought about how much bigger Prince had looked with his fur all fluffed up and standing on end. And that reminded her of something. "Ross? On Midsummer's Eve when you were striding around on the beach, posturing to the crowd, were you shape-shifting yourself to look bigger and scarier?"

"Aye, I suppose I was. I didn't expect quite so many onlookers. When I saw them, I figured I'd give them a tale to pass down to their grandchildren."

"If you can shape-shift the Zrakon body to be bigger than it is, can you also make it smaller than it is?"

He considered for a moment, and then started to grin. "You're asking me to downsize the Zrakon's dick?"

"Can you?"

"Admittedly, I've never tried."

She rolled her eyes. "Like any male would ever try to make his penis smaller."

He laughed. "It makes sense that if I can make him bigger, I ought to be able to shrink him. I suppose that if I shift his entire body to about human male size.... Hmm. What do I get in return?"

"How about my eternal gratitude?"

He laughed. "It's a deal."

"In that case, I'll do it. I'll be your sacrificial victim. Just try not to kill me, okay?"

He looked surprised. And touched. "Are you sure? Because, as much as I'm burning for you, I don't want to force you."

"I'm going to consider it a great adventure. And who knows, maybe someday someone will make up a myth about you and me."

Ross pulled her to him and kissed her. He started glowing, more brightly than ever, and she backed away.

"Damn. Let's get this over with," he growled.

Chapter Fifteen

The descending path snaked and twisted, but with Ross to guide their way, Kate was not worried about getting lost. She could smell the briny tang of the sea, and the air was fresh, suggesting an outlet to the outside world. As they squeezed through a narrow opening, he held his electric lantern high. Light flashed all around them, bouncing and shimmering from one reflective surface to the next. It was beautiful—like a magnification of the sparks that shimmered on Ross's body every time she got too close to him.

But what she was seeing was natural. They had entered a roughly circular cavern. The sea was rushing in from somewhere below, and all around them were jagged rock faces embedded with chunks of crystal. The light from the lantern was sparkling from thousands of crystal facets, shimmering in new patterns as the lantern moved.

The effect was breathtakingly beautiful. But she was so intent on gazing at the gleaming crystals that she tripped over some stones on the ground.

He caught her, and his arm grabbing her around the waist felt hot as a brand. He quickly let her go. "You see why I didn't want you to come here alone."

"I remember it. I was here before. It's where he brought me."

She continued to walk ahead of him down the narrow path that circled the pool. "It's a lovely spot for a sea dragon's den. I take it the water is coming in through an opening somewhere?"

"Yes. It's tidal. The tide is out now. It's beginning to turn, actually, but high tide is still several hours away." He joined her on the lip of the pool. "The pool is quite deep, even at low tide, and it's tidal, too. It will fill and overflow. At high tide, this cave will be full of water."

She looked up. The crystal ceiling was maybe two feet above their heads. "Entirely full?"

"Just about. You wouldn't want to be in here when the tide is high."

"What's that?" she asked, squinting at a rock platform on the far side of the cavern. It was the only place in the cave wall where the crystal chunks were sparse, and there was something strange there, something dark and jarring. She didn't remember seeing it on the night the Zrakon had brought her here.

"That," he said, "is where we're going. Come, I'll show you." Slipping carefully past her, he led the way down the still descending path towards the massive rock.

For a moment, she hesitated. As they got closer, she could see that there were two thick, sturdy-looking chains hammered into the rock wall. Each was several feet long, ending in a cruel iron manacle.

"Damn," she said.

"Indeed." He jumped down to the sandy bottom, which was about a couple of feet lower than the path she was standing on. There were several inches of water there now; he splashed through it to stand with his back against the rock. "You put the victim here and chain her to the rock." He was between the two chains. "When the tide is out, it's just a bit uncomfortable. But when the tide is full and the cavern floods..." he let his voice trail off.

"But the sea dragon comes before that happens, right? I mean, he's not going to let me drown."

"Of course not."

She ran her fingers over one of the chains. She would have expected it to be old and rusted, but it was shiny and new. She shivered. Had it been installed especially for her?

When she turned to look at Ross, he was glowing with a sparkling nimbus all around him. "Is that energy hurting you?"

"No. It's just very hard for me to maintain control."
His voice shook, and she believed him. "We may have
waited too long."

"Let's be quick about it then," she said practically.

She stripped off her clothing and jumped down to
join him. She tried not to look too hard at the depth of
the water in the cavern, which was rising rapidly. It
was as if the waves were responding to the tumult inside Ross.

When she reached the rock, she turned so her back
was against it. "You don't need to chain me. I won't
run away."

He was staring at her naked body. He seemed transfixed by the sight of her. "I'd better follow the ritual
exactly. I don't want to make him any angrier than he
already is. Are you frightened?"

She began to say no, but in all honesty, she was
frightened. She was trying not to think about what was
going to happen. Not thinking about it made it easier
to cope. "I am, of course. But I've met your Zrakon. He
was gentle with me."

"You met me wearing his shape. I was in control.
The beast wasn't dominant. Tonight he will be. He is
hungry. Angry at being denied. Frustrated at being
forced to wait. I'm not sure what he is going to do. All I
know is that he's bursting out of me and I can no longer rein him in."

"Okay then. Let's not make him wait any longer."

Ross took one of the chains and stretched it out. The heavy clank of iron rang an unpleasant note in the cavern. He hesitated. "You must be willing. I have to ask. It's part of the ritual."

"I am willing." She held out her wrists. "You see? I am giving myself to you."

His eyes seemed to glow a deeper blue. "You're so fucking brave. So positive and cheerful, too. You're bringing light into my darkness, you know?" He paused for a beat, and then added, "I'm in love with you."

She was so surprised, she didn't know how to respond. She blinked, feeling unaccountably teary. But she couldn't cry. Not now. He might think she was unwilling if she started blubbering, but that wasn't it at all. He was so strange and special. So sweet in so many ways. And so ferocious in others.

He touched her carefully. The glow retreated away from his hands, so they did not burn her. He took the first chain and crossed her body with it, from shoulder to hip. He put the iron manacles about her right wrist where it lay against her hip, then did the same on the other side. The manacles were loose on her, but as soon as they were closed, they seem to tighten of their own accord until she could feel the metal biting into her wrists. She shivered. There was real magic here. She could feel it. It seemed to pulse all around them, and it had a dark and ominous feel. This was not benign magic. This was ruthless, powerful, and fierce.

Ross stood back, looking at her chained to the rock. The water was now over her knees, which was scary because no tide could come in so fast. Ross didn't seem to notice. He was breathing hard. The glow around him intensified and became fiery. Maybe the sea dragons of Mallochbirn maintained some vestige of their dragon fire, after all.

"What now?"

He didn't speak. His eyes had gone wild. He began pulling at his clothing, shedding it rapidly, tearing it off. He seemed to waver before her eyes. His body emerged, strong and muscular. Even more muscular than usual, perhaps. He was beautiful. Between his thighs, his cock rose hard and thick and long. At least it doesn't have spikes on it, she thought, a little frantically.

The Hunger. She could feel the lust rolling off him. He stepped back toward her, the fiery glow hot and searing.

"No," she cried. "You can't touch me as a man. You must let yourself change."

He wavered, as if no longer sure what he was doing. "Ross," she thought it to him this time, trying to open the golden tunnel into his mind. "Can you hear me? You have to let the change happen."

The mental bond didn't form. It felt as though he was blocked off from her.

He turned from her and dived naked into the pool, which was already overflowing. The water was now splashing up over her hips, rising higher every second. The dark waves closed over his form and he disappeared.

Chapter Sixteen

"Ross...Zrakon...can you hear me?"

The water kept getting deeper. He had said that the cavern could flood, but only at high tide. Maybe a gale had swept in from the sea and sent more water crashing into the cave? It had been a calm, clear evening when they had begun to make their way down here.

But that was in another world. Here, in this world tinged and vibrating with magic, a storm was brewing. The waves were rolling, cresting. A harsh wind was blowing thru the cavern, sweeping her hair in ribbons around her. Oddly, it didn't feel cold. The rising water, which surely must derive from the cold Scottish seas outside, was cool but not icy.

Nothing about this made sense.

Where was Ross? He hadn't surfaced since he'd dived into the water. Had he transformed into the Zrakon? What if he'd drowned? No man could hold his breath for such a long time. Just as she wouldn't be able to hold hers if the damn water didn't stop coming in. Maybe they were both going to drown. Maybe that was what their doomed union was meant to be—a union in death. Maybe someone would find both their bodies washed up on the rocky shores of Mallochbirn Isle.

Then she heard the hissing. She had heard it before, a few nights ago in the surf near the village. The Zrakon. He was coming. He was coming for her.

Okay, where was her vaunted courage? This was all too freaky, with the wind and the waters, which were up to her waist already. "Ross?" She was sending out the golden thread, trying to reach his mind, but the thread was just flailing around. She couldn't find him; couldn't form the mental bond. She felt abandoned and alone.

The Zrakon was here, though. He hadn't surfaced, but he was racing round and round the cavern in a frenzy, occasionally flipping his mighty tail. Even though she could not communicate directly with the creature, she could sense his feelings. Lust. Triumph. Exultation. My god, what a male—he was delirious with the thrill of finally capturing his prey. Her.

"Zrak," she sent, determined to speak to him even if he was too stubborn to listen, "Calm down. Yes, I'm here and yes, you're about to achieve your goal. You're a mighty sea monster. Really kick-ass." She tried to sound as emotionally sincere as possible, sending all the praising, admiring, wow-you-are-excellent vibes she could manage.

"But you still have stuff to do here. Like freeing me from this rock before the water comes up over my head, which it's already doing every time your wake hits me. Stop that! Dammit, Zrak, I'm going to drown!"

Just as she was beginning to lose hope that he would ever quiet down, the waves stopped churning. She was chest deep in water now, and she was beginning to feel chilled. "Ross, for god's sake!" She writhed against the rock, trying to pull herself free of the chains. She knew it wasn't possible; they were too strong, but her body wasn't listening to reason. "If you're anywhere in there with a working *brain*, please help me!"

She felt something then. In her mind. Not a thought, exactly, but a warm and reassuring emotion. Or maybe she was imagining it. Maybe she was already drowning. Everything was so confusing with the magic vibrating around her, messing with her head.

She heard a roar, and the water rose up before her like a tidal wave. *This is it. I'm going to die.* But it was him, the Zrakon, lifting his snout out of the black sea. She saw his shiny scales and his piercing silver eyes. He opened his enormous mouth and roared again, all but puncturing her eardrums.

"Zrak! Stop that. I get it. You're awesome. Now get me out of these fucking chains!"

One of his mammoth paws swatted at her. She cringed involuntarily, expecting to feel a slash, but his claw only struck the chain, ripping one away from her body. Her arm with the manacle came up and she feared for her wrist, but the metal parted as he yanked it away. The pain was minimal. He seized the other chain and disposed of it in the same manner.

Thank god. She struggled to move to higher ground when one of the thick tentacles wrapped around her chest and waist. It was warm, as she remembered from the last time. But he was rougher than he'd been when Ross was in control. He jerked her against his chest, where the cage of tentacles had sheltered her when they swam together through the dark. Was he going to take her somewhere again? This was his lair, surely. Weren't they going to stay here?

He forced her against him, face first. She couldn't breathe. Her mouth and nose were plastered against hard, briny muscle. She tried to find the bud that would channel his air from his lungs, but he was holding her so roughly that movement was impossible.

"Ross!" she screamed in her head, still seeking the mental link that had become so elusive. Why couldn't she reach him?

There was a sharp pain in her scalp as Zrakon fingers yanked at her hair. But he was shifting her position. He jerked her neck back then slammed her into him again, and this time she felt the stubby protrusion that she recognized from the first time as the air bud. He pressed her face onto it, and she was able to get her mouth around it. Once again, it felt like a short, thick cock. Air rushed into her lungs and she breathed deeply.

He was being so rough!

Do that thing with your tongue again, she heard in her head. *He likes that.*

"Ross?" She nearly wept from pure thankfulness at hearing his familiar voice in her head.

He's letting me through, finally. Maybe he needs my sexual expertise.

To her surprise, he sounded amused. Lighthearted even. Relief rushed through her. Ross was here. He was still part of the Zrakon, even if his beast was dominant. Surely he wouldn't let anything horrible happen to her.

With his consciousness came his emotions—sweeping through her like the wind. Most of all, the Hunger. It was more than a man's lust—it was a primal storm of need and desire. Like the light from the lantern, it seemed to radiate around the cavern, from crystal to crystal, infinitely magnified.

She focused on her task—oral stimulation of a body part she couldn't even name. She ran her tongue around the edges of the appendage, then moved inward, trying to breathe at the same time that she darted her tongue into the soft, inside rim of the breathing slit. The Zrakon thrashed against her, and she heard the gleeful splash of his tail.

He readjusted her against him, and, between her legs, she felt the huge pressure of his mammoth thorny penis. Well, they weren't thorns, exactly. More like fleshy protrusions. One of them flexed and tickled her a little down there. Hmm, that could be interesting. It might be *very* interesting if it were considerably smaller than its current dimensions.

She hoped Ross would remember his plan to downsize the Zrakon. So far, the creature was just as huge as ever.

"What else does he like?" She reached one hand down to explore the scary penis. Maybe she could make friends with it?

Ah. Yesss, he said as she ran her fingers over the rounded tip. *He likes that. He likes that a lot.* The tip of a tentacle swished between her legs, and she jumped. He twisted in the water, his huge mouth opening wide, showing his fearsome teeth. She backpedaled furiously, but his tentacle held her. His big body flexed, and she realized he was stretching. Maybe even preening for her.

Can you convince him to let you keep talking to me? It'll be nicer for him if he lets you tell me what he wants.

That worked, Ross's amused voice responded a few seconds later. *He's going to let me guide you.*

"Jeez, this feels like a kinky threesome. With tentacles."

Because the water made her buoyant, she was able to twist a bit and float. She pulled on the massive prick, figuring she couldn't actually hurt the thing, until a good portion of it was above the surface of the water. She caressed him, moving her hand up and down the massive shaft. Did he enjoy that?

A watery gasp from his dragon mouth hinted strongly at his delight. It was strange, but the more she stroked him, the more his member began to feel similar to a human penis—the shape, the dimensions, the smoothness—everything. She backed away a little so she could look at it. Yes. Human. She blinked. Was it Ross beside her in the water? Was he shifting back to his human form?

Just as she thought he might be, an aura flashed and he was a sea dragon again. She squinted, confused. The fleshy barbs on his phallus started a couple inches down from the tip and descended the entire length of the shaft—a length she didn't even try to measure because it would totally freak her out. The width was formidable enough, without factoring in the length.

Again, she ran the palm of her hand down the shaft. The protrusions didn't hurt her. But they were so heavily concentrated that they made the organ even thicker than it already was. As she stroked them, the Zrakon made a deep crooning sound. Was he purring?

"This is so strange. Does it feel good to you?"

It's incredible. Has anyone ever told you how amazing you are?

"Me? You're the amazing one. I'm just an ordinary human."

She felt a surge, and the Zrakon gathered her in his arm-like appendages and lifted her out of the water. Striding forward on his hind legs, he carried her to the fine sand at one end of the cavern. He set her down carefully. The extra volume of water in the cavern was receding. The Zrakon might be horny as hell still, but at least he seemed calmer.

"You're lovely," he said aloud, his deep hissing voice echoing throughout the cavern.

She shook out her long, wet hair. "Thank you."

Ah, Catriona. This has been the longest week of my life. You are willing?

She was hearing Ross's inner voice and looking into the eyes of a lustful sea dragon who planned to take her for his mate. How this could happen, she still didn't understand.

"Yes."

Forgive me. I don't think I can be patient any longer.

What was she supposed to do? Remembering her dreams, she sat in the sand. If she lay down and spread herself out, would he crawl between her legs like a man, the way he had done in the dreams? And if he did, how could she possibly accommodate him? "Tell me what to do."

I'd shift into human form and hug you if I could, but I can't touch you that way. I can't seem to change, either. Not tonight. The Zrakon form is totally dominant.

At least they could communicate. How much more frightening it would be, she thought, if there were silence between them.

He stepped closer to her. As the water slid off his tough hide, his scales flashed bits of color, reflecting the crystals of the cave. He looked beautiful in a way. Proud and shining, this old dragon of yore. What had the Zrakon done, she wondered, that had lost him his place in the skies and reduced his magnificent wings to tatters?

She stretched out her hand. "Come. Tell me how to please a sea dragon."

Let me touch you. Don't be afraid.

"I'm not. Not anymore."

He stood straighter, but he seemed less huge. Was Ross shape shifting him downwards at last? He still towered over her, but not by so great a margin. His body changed in a subtle manner, becoming more human, less dragony. His face relaxed and even his eyes changed. The silver was still the dominant hue, but she could see some of Ross's blue in those eyes now, too.

He knelt down beside her. One of the tentacles from his pectoral region curled gently around her. The tip of another swished between her legs. It explored, caressing the petals of her labia. Some of the Hunger moved into her.

The ancient customs demand that I stay in the Zrakon form for the mating. Shape shifting downwards in size will take magical energy, but I will sustain it as long as I can. Ultimately, though, I fear I am going to have to hurt you."

Kate reached out towards his head, and he brought her closer. She stroked the leathery skin around his large eyes. "A little sexy pain is okay," she said, trying to be lighthearted about it.

"Catriona. The voice in her head was tender now. *Tonight is for you and me. I just wish I didn't have to spend it as a reptile."*

She smiled. "You're a mammal, remember?"

"Right. Well that's different, then." He was laughing. *"Still, I won't be offended if you close your eyes."*

"I don't need to close my eyes." She put her arms around his scaly neck. "In fact, I'm beginning to find this new body of yours rather interesting, Zrak. Are you going to show me what else you can do with your tentacles?"

This body has all sorts of unique surprises in store for you, beloved. I don't believe you've yet been introduced to my long, agile tongue."

She laughed. "This telepathy thing is awesome. It's so cool to hear you in my head. No matter what you look like on the surface, I know it's you. It's too bad more people don't see the inside of their lover, rather than just their outward form."

So true. But you're beautiful, inside and out.

She felt the Hunger thunder through the cavern— through the very world, it seemed—as he began to arouse her with those amazing tentacles and that flexible tongue, using his dear, familiar voice in her mind every bit as much as he used his strange, unfamiliar body.

In the end, as promised, he made himself only a little taller and broader than she, but his barbed phallus still seemed to her like a torture instrument from one of the Inquisition's darkest dungeons. His body was much closer now to a man's size, but his dick was still enormous.

Despite the desire he had nurtured in her, as she lay back and opened herself to him, she feared she would soon be screaming in pain. She had heard there were ways to savor erotic pain, as long as it was mixed with the right amount of pleasure. She could endure, she told herself, even if there were no rewards to be harvested.

He crouched over her. *Kate, forgive me, I must—I have to—*

"It's all right. I'm ready, take me."

She felt pressure and a burst of pain, nothing close to her limits at first, then rising sharply. The knobby protuberances rammed against her soft tissues, trying to force their way inside her. It was agonizing. She tried her best to relax, but this was almost impossible against such an assault. But just as it was beginning to seem intolerable, there were sparks all around him and a powerful glow of magic that flashed throughout the cavern from crystal to crystal, bathing them both in shining rainbows of light.

She felt him slide inside her with no pain, his movements transformed into strokes of smooth, frictionless delight. His scales dissolved into flesh, and his silvery sea dragon eyes turned cornflower blue. Instead of tentacles, Ross's hair tickled her body, and she could feel his warm human skin, sinew, and bone.

"Oh, Ross."

Her willingness to accept the Zrakon and take his alien flesh inside her must have broken the spell. His human form was no longer banned from touching her. He was Ross again.

"Kate, thank god," he spoke to her in his real, human voice. "Are you all right? It doesn't hurt?

"No, no, not at all."

His mouth lowered to hers at last, and he kissed her as their bodies joyfully fulfilled the unspoken promise that had been made between them when two strangers had looked into each other's eyes and felt the Mallochbirn magic jolt them.

His cock still stretched her, but it was a delicious pressure now, and she arched her back to meet him thrust for thrust. He went deep, touching something inside her that sent her pleasure spiraling ever higher. She held on tightly to the driving muscles on his back, loving the way they flexed every time he moved.

"I love you, Kate," he said, gasping the words, but managing a crooked smile.

"I love you, too." It was true, she realized. She grinned back as his mouth came down to kiss her long and hard. She had fallen in love with a shape shifting sea dragon, somehow making her way into the very folklore she'd always loved to read.

Her monster slid one hand under her and tilted her pelvis so his cock put pressure on her clit with each thrust. The combination of his fierce penetration and this extra stimulation soon wound her up to the breaking point. Her muscles clenched around his shaft and the warmth in her belly tightened and spread throughout her body, racing along all her nerves to flood her with the most intense bliss she had ever experienced.

She cried out as she crested the wave. Such exquisite pleasure. With her tissues throbbing around him, he slammed into her a few more times before he stiffened and groaned as he emptied himself deep inside her.

Around them, the colors danced as the crystals shone.

Chapter Seventeen

Kate woke one morning three months later with the sun in her eyes and her lover's voice in her mind:

It's time to play, beloved.

Feeling an odd sensation, she opened her eyes. A large butterfly beat his wings rapidly against her toes, then flew up and landed on her stomach. She saw brightly-colored, diaphanous wings of near-transparency and great beauty. "You're gorgeous," she said. "Good morning, my laird."

He flew out of her line of sight. Something growled. A large, sleek mountain lion was standing beside the bed. He licked one of her breasts with a rough tongue. She gasped, and then giggled. Reaching out, she patted his head, and then rubbed along the side of his jaw. He started purring. She stroked the soft hair behind his ear and laughed when he head-butted her palm.

"I hope you've already had your breakfast."

You know what I'm hungry for.

He shrank and twisted before her eyes and became a snake. He flowed over her body, arrowed down across the expanse of her belly, coiled around her thighs. His head found her and a tiny, delicate tongue flicked across her sex. She moaned.

"You're a very wicked man, er, magical creature."

Ha. I will show you wicked. He became a mosquito and settled on her thigh; considered, humming his high-pitched whine, then flew up and landed threateningly on her nipple.

"What if I swat you? Will all forms of you die?"

He turned into an owl and perched on her hand, looking very thoughtful and wise. *That, my love, is an interesting question. I don't know. I have a feeling that if you—or anyone else—tried to injure me, I could simply shape-shift the injury until it healed. But if I were instantly snuffed out, I guess I wouldn't have the time to do so. So don't swat me, please.*

She reached down with her free hand to stroke his feathers. "In that case, you'd better not do anything that makes it tempting to swat you."

He became a very long snake who rapidly coiled himself around her torso several times, imprisoning her arms inside his tight coils. *Can't swat me now.* His head aimed downward and flicked her between her legs again.

Kate closed her eyes. She had always liked snakes. But she was glad when he turned into Ross again, a very eager, human Ross whose ability to keep teasing her was lost in his own need.

They made love languorously, taking the time to fully enjoy one another. Afterwards, she asked, "Can you be any creature you choose, now?"

"Some are harder than others—I don't know why. And some take more of my energy than others do. Winged creatures in particular are exhausting."

"What's the easiest?"

The bed groaned beneath them, and scaly knobby hide was all she could see or feel. He had transformed into the Zrakon. His tail dragged on the floor, taking up much of the room in the bedchamber. His deep voice hissed out. "This form takes no special energy and is easy to maintain."

"Easier than your human form?"

"No. Human is still the most natural."

"You know, you've never confirmed whether there are other shape shifters in your family. Does your twin do this sort of thing too?"

"My twin does all sorts of strange things."

"Well, that's vague!"

"Why do you want to know about him?"

She gave him a lusty grin. "Well, hey. Guys have twin fantasies, right? Can't a girl indulge a dream about two extremely hot guys taking her together?"

"Certainly not," he growled. "You're mine. No way that reprobate is getting near you."

"You're all I really want," she said, laughing. Stroking the Zrakon's scales she added, "My love, you're going to destroy the bed."

He shifted back to human Ross. "I wouldn't want to do that. Especially since that bed is cradling not only my beloved wife, but also my child."

"Your child is nothing more than a speck at the moment, love."

He kissed her bare belly. "Such a lively little speck. I swear I can feel him moving around in there."

She laughed. "It's probably gas. But in a few weeks, we should both be able to feel him. Or her."

He slid up to kiss her mouth, while she tangled her fingers in his hair. "Are you happy, Catriona?"

"Deliriously happy."

"I love you."

She caressed his hair. She didn't think she would ever get enough of his long, lithe body, his silky hair, his sea blue eyes. But her love encompassed so much more than that now. His shape shifting ability had forced her to look deeper, and the telepathic connection had made this easy. She knew and loved the real Ross Malloch. The lively mind and generous spirit who dwelt beneath all his various surfaces. "You'd better. I tamed your monster, didn't I?"

"Aye, you surely did."

"I love you, too, Ross. Zrak. Tentacles and all."

"I think you love my tentacles more than the rest of me."

"I do not."

"Oh aye? I say you do. Shall we test my theory? We could go down to the cavern and splash around."

She laughed. "Any time, Zrak. Any time."

THE END

ABOUT THE AUTHOR

Linda Barlow is the bestselling author of 23 novels, with more on the way. She lives in New England with her mysterious spouse (who sleeps during the day, which has often made her wonder if he's a vampire) and their equally enigmatic and nocturnal cat.

Her novel *Leaves of Fortune* won the Rita Award, and *Fires of Destiny* was a finalist for the same award. She loves reading, writing, computer games, and dark chocolate.

For information on how to purchase her other titles, please visit her website at: www.lindabarlow.com.